For the Life of Laetitia

MERLE HODGE

A Dolphin
Paperback

Published in paperback in 1996

First published in Great Britain in 1995
by Orion Children's Books
a division of the Orion Publishing Group Ltd
Orion House
5 Upper St Martin's Lane
London WC2H 9EA

First published in the United States under the title,
For the Life of Laetitia, Merle Hodge.
Copyright © Merle Hodge 1993.
Published by arrangement with
Farrar Straus & Giroux.

A catalogue record for this book is available
from the British Library

Typeset by Datix International Limited, Bungay, Suffolk
Printed in England by Clays Ltd, St Ives plc

ISBN 1 85881 253 4

for Marjorie Thorpe

When we set out down the Trace that morning, I wasn't feeling too joyful. It was very strange to be going down Sooklal Trace in a motorcar. People stopped whatever they were doing in their yards and peered at us. Some were taking water from their barrels at the side of the road, washing clothes, or bathing. Some waved, or looked puzzled when they recognized me.

The car was old, and it made a lot of noise over the bumps and holes in the road. The worst part was that my father kept trying to make conversation with me above the noise.

'So you like plenty books, eh? Well, we will see what we can do. I have one or two books myself, you know.'

He was very impressed with the box of books I had put into the car along with the suitcase.

'I like a little reading now and then, you know. Although I wasn't so bright as you – I didn't get pick to go to secondary school. I only make it to seventh standard.'

He kept turning his head to grin at me, and I thought that sooner or later he would run into some-body's barrel. Sooklal Trace had never seemed so long, even though I was travelling in a car. It seemed much longer than when I walked out on mornings with the other schoolchildren, or when I got a bumpy ride on the bar of Uncle Leroy's bike.

'I tell your brother, I say: "Well, you see what your sister do? She come and she pass her exam for secondary school. Well, you know what you have to do now – you can't let the girls beat you!"' And with this he laughed from down in his belly, glancing at me again and again to see if I was enjoying the joke.

He was still laughing when he passed Miss Adlyn going down the road with the baby. The boy was all dressed up, and I knew she was taking him to the clinic in La Puerta for his regular checkup. She heard the car coming and put out her hand to beg for a lift. When she realized we were not going to stop, she paused to shift the baby over to the shoulder where the bag was, and the bag over to the other shoulder.

I couldn't even wave at her – I wanted to sink down into the car seat. I could imagine Miss Adlyn making her way down the Trace, changing around the baby and the bulging bag several times before she got to the main road. There she would wait in the shade of Rampie's shop for a bus, maybe give up after an hour and pay the taxi fare to Junction, then in Junction wait again for a bus to La Puerta. And we were going to La Puerta!

'But your Tantie Velma will help you with your lesson. Yes, man, she is the one in the family with

2

education. She was a high-school girl, too, you know!' He glanced over at me again and looked back just in time to swerve away from Mr Popo's dog, sunning itself in the middle of the Trace. He cursed the dog under his breath, then put on his smile again.

'Yes, man, she just waiting to measure you up for your uniform.'

This brightened me a little. I began to feel excited about school again.

The government secondary school was the biggest and most modern thing in La Puerta. I used to look at it with awe when I went with Ma and Carlyle to sell the cocoa. It was not one building, but several, and all of them two storeys high.

I looked at the students with awe, too: the way they took over the streets in their plaid uniforms, talking and laughing gaily, as if they owned the town.

And now I had been given a place at this school! My name was right there in the newspapers, among all the other children who had passed the Common Entrance Examination: JOHNSON, LAETITIA CHRISTINA. It was a Sunday, and Uncle Jamesie was home for the day with Tantie Monica and the children. Pappy right away sent Uncle Leroy out the road to knock on Rampie's side door for a bottle of rum and some sweet drinks.

I would be the first one ever, the first one in the family to go to secondary school. Pappy made speech after speech about the new and blessed day that was dawning in the land. The celebration went on until Uncle Jamesie realized that darkness would catch them walking out the Trace if they didn't leave in a hurry. By then even Ma was tipsy, dancing with us one by one.

Two days later my father appeared, out of the blue. He, too, was bursting with pride.

I had never seen much of my father before this. We spotted him now and then on our trips into La Puerta, and if he saw me, he would call me over and begin to fish in his pockets until he found a dollar bill. He would press the money into my hand and say: 'Go and buy sno-cone.'

Sometimes Uncle Leroy got a few days' road work in Junction, and if my father passed that way and saw him, he might give Uncle Leroy five dollars for me. One Christmastime he sent a present, a doll in a white and gold dress, and my mother said it must be the Christmas rum in his head.

Ma, my grandmother, did not have a very high opinion of him. Whenever we met him in town, she would grumble all the way back home on the bus, every now and then stopping to suck her teeth loudly: '*Steups!* Anyhow, the less said about that man the better.'

But before a few minutes had passed she would begin to grumble again about how he had no conscience, and how he would meet his Judgement Day. She complained that now he was a big Supervisor, driving motorcar and all, and still wouldn't help his child in a decent and proper manner.

'Sno-cone?' she said. 'The child could live on sno-cone?'

And then again she would stop and chide herself: 'Look, Wilhemina Johnson, hush your old mouth. Less said, the better. Leave him to God. Hah! He will meet his Judgement, so help me he will meet it.'

You can imagine, then, that when my father appeared in front of our house that day, for the first time in many years, my grandmother did not greet him warmly to begin with. He arrived with the back seat of his car full of parcels, which turned out to be presents for me, to reward me for having passed my exam.

At first he just sat out in the car, not knowing what to do, for Ma was standing in the doorway, her two hands on her hips, regarding him with a face of stone.

He grinned nervously and waved a limp hand. 'Good afternoon, Ma Willie.'

Ma sent Carlyle to invite him in. The other children were only waiting for her to move from the doorway in order to run down the path and swarm all over the car. And quite a swarm we were, for it was August vacation, and in addition to the children who lived here all the time (Ruth and Kenwyn, Carlyle, and myself) we had Uncle Leroy's daughter Charlene, one of Ma's godchildren, Carlyle's little brother, and two of Uncle Jamesie's children who had refused to go back to Petit-Fort with their parents on Sunday. But Ma knew what was in their minds: 'All of you, find yourself in the back yard!' she snapped. 'Lacey, you come inside.'

So the three of us sat in the drawing room. Pappy and Uncle Leroy were down in the cocoa.

My father said he wanted me to come and stay with him and his family in La Puerta, now that I would be going to school there. He'd been walking around with the newspaper in his pocket. He had opened a bottle of whisky for the fellows on the job. He had shown the Big Boss my name in the paper, and told him that I was his daughter, and the Big Boss had congratulated him.

My father could hardly contain himself.

'Ma Willie,' he said, 'let me do my duty as a father.'

Ma gave a dry laugh that stayed in her throat. But she knew – as I did – that going to live in the town would make life a lot easier for me. La Puerta meant nearly two miles on foot to begin with, and then about four miles to Balatier Junction by bus or taxi, and the long bus ride to La Puerta. It would mean leaving home at some ungodly hour in the morning, and getting back only just before dark.

Also, nobody had as yet counted up what it would cost in fares. Uncle Leroy said that I could get a student's bus pass to ride free on the bus; but the buses along this part of the main road were not very regular, so on mornings I would very likely have to take a taxi to Junction. And we didn't have money to pay taxi fare every day of the week.

Ma questioned my father closely. What did his wife think of my coming to live there? Did he intend to buy my books and uniform? Would he see to it that I didn't run wild in the town and get myself into trouble like so many of these high-school girls nowadays?

My father nodded vigorously to everything: 'Yes, Ma Willie! Of course, Ma Willie! . . .'

When the interrogation was over, she still didn't give him much of an answer. She told him that we would have to write to my mother first, and I would have to ask my grandfather, and my uncles.

He left, looking a little downcast. Ma told him that Uncle Leroy would bring a message to him at his workplace.

Pappy gave another long speech. There comes a time in every man's life, he said, when he repenteth of the evil he hath done. That time was come for my father; he was repenting of his deeds. No man can walk in waywardness for all the days of his life.

Uncle Leroy cut in to say that he didn't mind my going to live in La Puerta, as long as I came home on weekends to clean his bicycle. Pappy roared at him to stop making damn jokes, this was not a time for joking. Uncle Leroy wiped the grin off his face and cleared his throat, winking at me.

Ma was pretending that she had no opinion on the matter and that she was letting the rest of us decide. But I knew that she had made up her mind, even before my mother, Mammy Patsy, wrote back to say that she approved.

... It is high time that man do something for the child. If he will help to support her then maybe I can soon give up mopping the dirty hospital floor and come home to my garden.

I am so glad that Lacey got her place in secondary school. It is a weight off my mind. For otherwise I would have had to bring her up here to get some education, and that is the last thing I want to do. I wouldn't want to bring a dog in this New York. Ruth and Kenwyn had better see about passing their exam, too, when the time comes, because I don't want to have to send for any of them. Not a child of mine must have to come and live this life. This place they call New York is not fit for people, far less for people's children. So those other two had better study their lessons, for their father is no big-shot and can't help them much. As loving and willing as Kenneth might be, you know that he has little more to his name than the hair on his head and the pants on his backside.

I heard from him last week. He told me how he took the children to spend a few days by his mother and how Mr Kenwyn nearly killed the poor old lady with running about and jumping up on her lap and asking a million questions. And she so glad to see them that she found the strength to keep up with them. I wrote to Kenneth that he must take them to see her more often, for I don't think Ma Charlotte is long for this world, and they must know her, and she must have the satisfaction of her grandchildren.

Lacey can go and live with her father to go to school if he and his wife will treat her good. But if they show her any kind of bad face she must pack her bundle and go straight back home. I would just have to stay and mop the hospital until I see every one of them through.

I am posting a barrel soon. Tell Leroy that as soon as it comes he must take the two little dresses to Charlene before they get too small for her. I bought the same size for her and Ruth, but I don't know if they are still neck and neck. These children grow so fast. Lacey must send me a picture of herself in her high-school uniform . . .

10

When Uncle Jamesie and Tantie Monica came up again, they were told of my father's offer. They, too, were glad that he was at last going to do something for me.

So it was decided. Late, late in the August vacation, Uncle Leroy said to me: 'But, Lacey, you ain't say nothing yet! You want to go?'

And I replied: 'Well, I tired cleaning your bicycle, Uncle Leroy, I think I going, yes.'

The two of us laughed loudly, as usual, at our own joke.

Ma took me to register at the school. It was even bigger than it seemed before, with long, high buildings ranged one behind the other, and a huge playing field stretching away until it was stopped by bush.

There were tables set up in a hall as big as the yard. A loud murmur filled the hall, but nobody in particular seemed to be making any noise. The children waiting with their big-people seemed quite cowed, and the big-people, too, seemed nervous and lost.

We were directed to a table behind which there sat a man and a woman. The man said 'Hello' very pleasantly; the lady did not look up. I thought to myself that she probably couldn't, what with all the weight she carried on her head.

She was wearing enormous gold earrings – they could have been little force-ripe oranges attached to her earlobes. She had too much hair for her thin face, and all of it was piled into a large bundle of rolls, stiff as wire and pulled to one side of her head. Her cheeks, her mouth, and her eyelids were plastered in three different colours of heavy grease: her cheeks in red, her mouth in maroon, and her eyelids in a greenish blue. We couldn't see the whole of her dress, but it was bright red and very stylish, and she was hung with beads and chains and bangles.

'Name?' she asked the paper in front of her.

'Laetitia Johnson.'

'Name of mother?'

'Patsy Johnson.'

'Name of father?'

'Orville Cephas.'

Now she raised her head for a second, to throw us a look of disgust.

'Address?'

I looked up at Ma, and silently we debated the question of what to give as my address.

'Address!' the woman fumed when a few seconds had passed.

Ma turned to her with the purse-lipped face she used when she wanted to remind us of our manners: 'Put *Sooklal Trace, Balatier*,' she said curtly.

The woman sucked her teeth – sucked her teeth at Ma! 'What you mean "*Put* Sooklal Trace, Balatier"? That is the child's address or not? You people always giving bogus information, and when something happen, nobody know where to find the parents . . .

'Miss!' Ma barked in a terrible voice.

'Take it easy, Mrs Lopez, take it easy,' said the man, putting aside the papers he was working on. 'Let me help you.' And he took the form from her.

'Okay, let's see now. You must be Laetitia's grandmother?'

Ma thawed out and smiled. 'Yes, sir, this is my daughter child.'

'And you responsible for her?'

'Yes, sir. My name is Mistress Wilhemina Johnson, and I am responsible for this child.'

'Right. So your address is Sooklal Trace, Balatier? That's what we want.'

The man filled out the whole form. The lady had washed her hands of us and sat with her head propped on her elbow, staring into space.

On the bus home Ma reviewed the events of the day, sometimes aloud, sometimes to herself, when I would only see her shake her head or suck her teeth.

Sometimes she smiled to herself. The outing had not been all a trial: after the registration Ma had visited her *macommère* in La Puerta, Ma Zelline, my mother's godmother. Ma could stay in town as long as she pleased, for Uncle Leroy was seeing about lunch for everybody at home.

As soon as we arrived, Ma began fretting to Ma Zelline about the unmannerliness of the woman at the school: '*Salope!*' she said indignantly. 'And if you see how it dress-up like a damn circus-horse!'

Ma Zelline said something in patois and the two of them held their waists and cackled scandalously. Ma soon put the unmannerly woman behind her and they went on to talk about everything under the sun, switching to patois whenever they had something to say that was not for my ears. All the while, Ma Zelline puffed away on her pipe.

We went out into the yard to admire Ma Zelline's flower garden. She had the most amazing orchids and anthuriums and her whole back yard was colour and beauty. Ma walked around, delightedly sniffing flowers and gathering cuttings.

In her front yard Ma Zelline grew ratchet and dasheen bush, which, to other people, really belonged in your back yard. The dasheen bush grew lawlessly, its big heart-shaped leaves darkening the little space between Ma Zelline's house and the road. Prickly ratchet plants stood like well-armed guards in their midst.

When we went inside, Ma Zelline served stout with milk, and I was deemed old enough to have some. We sat around the kitchen table and sipped. Ma looked quite relaxed, and Ma Zelline was only too pleased with her company.

'Well, allyu spending the day, not so?' Ma Zelline urged.

Ma looked a little doubtful.

'Willie,' said Ma Zelline. 'You always so hurry to run back to your old man in the bush. What happen, you 'fraid somebody thief him?' Then she slid into patois with a wicked expression on her face, and again they held their waists and bawled helplessly with laughter. All I could understand was *doux*, which meant 'sweet'. But I heard other words which I knew were only for big-people's conversation, not for children to understand.

Ma Zelline had neither chick nor child nor regret to rankle her old age, Ma used to say, for Zelline belonged to Zelline. And people were so damn *fas*, so out of order, that they had everything to say about her, and only because from since she was a young girl they couldn't tell her what to do and what not to do.

Late in the afternoon we set out for home with flowers and plants, a cake Ma Zelline had baked, and a book for me – a present for having passed my exam. It was a book about Marie Curie.

Ma Zelline always had something for me when Ma or Mammy Patsy took me to visit her. In her drawing room there was a beautiful polished bookcase. She said that when she died I was to have the whole thing, books and all.

Ma usually left Ma Zelline's house in a good mood. But today her good humour gave way to indignation every time she remembered the rude woman. 'Old *jamet*!' she would suck her teeth and mutter every now and then. 'Dress-up like a damn circus-horse!'

Ma agreed to let my father come for me one week before school opened. Uncle Leroy said, however, that I wasn't going anywhere unless I cleaned up my garden. He promised to take care of it for me while I was away, but only if I left it in a fit condition – not one single weed, and all the plants neatly moulded.

So I got up very early the day before I left, to weed and mould. Charlene, Ruth, and Kenwyn woke up, too, and came out with me.

It was so early that the chickens were only just stirring in the guava tree, coming to life one by one. Every now and then there would be a little fluttering and squawking, and a fowl would suddenly drop out of the tree with a thud, like a breadfruit. It would sit in a daze for a while, then shake its feathers and walk off with its wings raised as if to let in the air of the new day through all its pores.

Uncle Leroy was already down in the big garden. He was cutlassing an area to plant out some yam cuttings and plantain suckers, and as I worked I could hear the steady swish, swish of the swiper from down behind the starch mango tree. Uncle Leroy said it was a very good thing that I was going

17

to live somewhere else, for the way that Carlyle and I were eating these days, he would have had to plant up the whole of the land in order to feed the two of us.

The little children helped with all their might for ten minutes or so. They pulled a few weeds, and then set off to see what Uncle was doing. (His daughter, Charlene, called him 'Uncle,' too, like all the other children.) They would go and squat at a safe distance from the range of the swiper, among the dogs and puppies who always gathered nearby, and ask him questions in a steady stream. Uncle would stop working every few minutes to answer, until he'd had enough and chased them away.

It wasn't long before the children came cheerfully bouncing up the track once more, holding hands – like three blind mice, with a train of dogs and puppies behind them.

Next they headed for the plum tree, to pick all the ripe plums they could reach. I would have to make sure that I visited the tree, too, before Carlyle came out to clean the pigpen and feed the pigs. The plums were only just coming in, and after Carlyle made his raid there would be no point looking for any.

After some time Uncle Leroy came up to inspect my garden.

'All right,' he said, 'how this plantation going? Ready for the big harvest?'

Uncle Leroy always made fun of my little plot. He called me the 'Minister of Agriculture,' and said he was saving up to buy me a combine harvester for my birthday.

I made a face.

'But you have to harvest, Farmer Lacey. You have to carry some of your produce for your father!'

There was not much in my garden that you could call 'produce.' I had planted pigeon peas on Corpus Christi, and they had sprouted and grown very nicely; but they were still just pretty young plants that would not bear before Christmas. The bhaji and the pumpkin vine were flourishing. There were about three flowers along the pumpkin vine, still sheltering under leaves. Then I had ochroes. They were small and misshapen, twisted as if they were in pain, but still, they were ochroes.

'I could carry ochro and bhaji,' I said.

Uncle Leroy looked doubtful. 'Ochro maybe, but you think those people does eat bhaji? That is poor-people food, you know. High-class people does eat something name 'spinach.' Is the same, same thing. But! Spinach come from America. Bhaji is just bush that grow in we back yard.'

I picked some of my twisted ochroes, and Uncle Leroy later packed them into a box with other vegetables from the big garden, some of Ma's sugar-cakes and tamarind balls, and some big brown eggs, the best kind.

Uncle Leroy had said that my garden looked good enough, so I took up the hoe and fork and went to the shed to put them away. A strong smell of coffee was in the air. Ma and Pappy were out in the kitchen, making breakfast. They were talking in their humming, unhurried way, like a light, steady shower of rain on the roof. All my life, for as far back as I could remember, that was how the big-people in the house had talked together, especially at night when we children were already in bed. Ma, Pappy, Uncle Leroy, my mother, and Uncle Jamesie would sit in the gallery and chat. Or they would talk to each other through the partitions, my mother in the big bed with us, Ma and Pappy in their bedroom, and the uncles out in the drawing room, for that was where they used to sleep when I was little.

Listening to their voices at night always made me pleasantly drowsy, and I would fall asleep cradled in their conversation. Now, as I heard their chatting coming from the kitchen, I felt the same sweet drowsiness come over me, and the world felt good, and safe.

The long, uneasy drive to La Puerta had come to an end at last. My father was slowing down before his house. There was a driveway and garage, but he parked in the road.

His wife was sitting in a rocking chair in the gallery. We got out of the car and went up the steps and she was still sitting, rocking mournfully, with a *Daily Word* open on her lap. My father opened the little gate into the gallery and gave me a gentle push, for I was standing hesitant on the top step.

'Good morning, Mistress Cephas,' I said, according to Ma's instructions.

'Good morning, doo-doo,' she answered, smiling and mournful at the same time, and holding out her arms for me to approach.

Her head was tied with a pale cloth that made her seem to be sick or sorrowing. Yet her eyes were bright and curious, and as she took me in from head to toe, the sad little one-sided smile opened out into a broad, delighted grin.

'Well, when you vex with me you could call me Mistress Cephas,' she said, making a face. 'But as long as we ain't vex, I am Miss Velma.' And she squeezed my hands.

My father had meanwhile carried my suitcase and box of books inside the house, and now he was on his way out again.

'Coming back now, Velma,' he said over his shoulder as he went down the steps. His wife was getting up from the chair, and she waved him away without a glance in his direction, but muttering something under her breath.

We went inside, passing through the drawing room, which on that first day seemed a forest of furniture and ornaments. Miss Velma showed me into a bedroom.

In there was one neatly made bed, and one in an awful state. Miss Velma hurried over and tidied the tousled bed, complaining that she had already made it up twice for the day. She also pushed away some shoes and cars and a toy machine gun that were lying about on the floor.

'I don't know where that boy is,' she said. 'He don't stay home at all. Only come home to make mess in the place and then gone about his business again.'

She sucked her teeth with annoyance.

'Look, doo-doo,' she said, pointing to the other bed. 'You will sleep here.'

Miss Velma also showed me two shelves in the cupboard that had been cleared for me, and some empty hangers on one side of the wardrobe.

But I looked around the room and was not sure that I wanted to unpack anything. Not my books, for if this little boy were to meddle and damage any of them ... The little ones at home had learned to handle my books with care, even Kenwyn, whom Ma called 'The Destroyer'.

But this little boy ... Nobody living under the same roof as Ma could walk away and leave their bed in such a state! You wouldn't dream of it!

I put my box of books under the bed and then opened my suitcase. There weren't very many clothes to unpack, for Ma hadn't allowed me to bring anything that was old, or faded, or had any little hole or tear in it. And when those had been put aside, all that was left were three dresses, a skirt and two blouses, and a pair of trousers. I wasn't sure what I would wear for home clothes, because for some reason Ma wouldn't let me bring any shorts.

I unpacked the clothes and left all my other belongings in the suitcase, which I placed under the bed with my books. Meanwhile, Miss Velma had put out lunch for me. She had not set a place for herself, but while I ate she sat at the dining-room table and chatted.

Suddenly there was a lot of noise in the gallery: 'VOOM-VOOM! DRNN-DRNN! SKREEK!' and a shrimp of a boy burst into the drawing room, still 'driving' some loud vehicle.

He drove straight past us and into the bedroom.

'Michael!' said Miss Velma. She had to call him about three times before he came out. 'Your manners? You don't see somebody sitting down here?'

The boy rolled his eyes all over the place, pretending to search around the room, under the furniture, up on the ceiling.

'Michael! You going to say Hello to your sister, or you going to show your dirty colours?'

'What she name?' he asked casually and started to rev up his vehicle again.

'You *know* her name. I tell you already: Laetitia.'

'Okay, Lettuce. DRNN-DRNN! VVVVV!' And he headed for the bedroom again.

'Come and eat your lunch, na,' Miss Velma offered.

'Later, man, later. I tired,' came Michael's voice from the bedroom. Miss Velma shook her head and sank back on the chair.

I was glad that I had put my things away under the bed, although I was still a little nervous that he might go digging for them.

'Lettuce,' indeed! I decided that if I was going to be living here, I would have to squash this little boy as soon as possible and let him know where to get off with me. He would soon find out what to expect from Lettuce.

After I'd finished, I washed my plate in the kitchen. Miss Velma went to her room to lie down, and I went to the bedroom. Michael was on his bed playing with a car, and as he continued to ignore me, I didn't pay him any mind either.

There didn't seem to be much else to do but lie down. I pulled my box from under the bed to find a book. Michael immediately stopped playing and craned his neck to see what was in the box.

'What you watching?' I snapped at him. 'Mind your business. And if you touch anything here, you will see!'

I got a book out of the box and settled down on the bed to read. But the house was so quiet that I fell asleep.

When I woke up, it was nearly dark. I could hear

Miss Velma's voice coaxing Michael to eat. Michael's bed was nearly naked; half the sheet was trailing on the floor. Because Ma had reminded me again and again to 'help Mrs Cephas in the house', and because I felt sorry for Miss Velma leaning over and fixing this bed God knows how many times a day, I straightened the sheet.

But I decided that this Michael, before long, would learn to make his bed and tidy his belongings away.

Mr Cephas came home very late in the night. Miss Velma had sat all evening in the rocking chair with her *Daily Word* on her lap, craning her neck every time she heard a car. She finally got up with a long sigh and walked slowly, heavily through the house to her bedroom. She walked as though she were twice as old as Ma.

The next morning, very early, she woke me up to go to church with her. The church was a long walk away. By the time we got back, the sun was high in the sky.

Mr Cephas's car was parked snugly in the garage, and the house was still closed up and quiet as a tomb. Miss Velma opened the front door with great care, and since she tiptoed through the drawing room, so did I.

She changed her clothes and went to the kitchen. Michael was still sleeping, sprawled across the bed. When I had finished changing my clothes, I dragged the cover off him to wake him up.

In the kitchen Miss Velma was working on both breakfast and lunch. She had put the radio on the counter and was trying to listen to *Sunday Theatre*. Ma also enjoyed listening to this programme, but

Miss Velma had the radio turned down to the faintest possible volume, so it didn't seem to me that she could be getting much out of it.

Michael appeared at the kitchen door and announced peevishly that he was hungry. Miss Velma put us both to sit at the kitchen table and set food before us. Then, still straining her ears to hear the radio, she went to and fro between the kitchen and dining room, setting the big polished table for Mr Cephas.

Michael disappeared into the neighbourhood shortly after he'd eaten. His bed and the area surrounding it looked like what my mother would call the Wreck of the Hesperus. Mr Cephas woke up and Miss Velma turned up the radio, just in time to hear the last few words and the theme song of *Sunday Theatre*.

Before he sat down to eat, Mr Cephas put on a record of holy music. 'Nearer, my God, to Thee' blared through the house. Miss Velma turned off her little radio and started to cut up the chicken for lunch. She took her tea on her feet. At the end of 'Onward, Christian Soldiers' the music went off. Shortly afterwards Mr Cephas's car started up and drove out. We were peeling the vegetables.

Michael came home when he was hungry. Miss Velma had to fill him up with sweet-biscuits to keep him quiet, because Mr Cephas wasn't home yet for Sunday lunch. He finally arrived at a quarter past three and we sat down to lunch in a thunder of hymns. Mr Cephas kept putting meat on my plate and urging me to eat up, 'to boost the brain.'

Miss Velma and I cleared the table and washed the dishes. Mr Cephas went and polished his car for the next two hours with the hymns turned up full blast. Michael was nowhere to be seen.

I was sitting in the drawing room, reading. This drawing room still made me feel very uncomfortable and out of place. It was crammed with upright furniture, most of which was dressed in dark velveteen. There were crowds of ornaments everywhere, rich-looking ornaments that jostled each other on little tables, on the walls, and on the big television set that was out of order. This drawing room was like the store windows you saw in town, not a place where you would go and sit in your home clothes.

But Ma had instructed me that in Other People's House I could not spend hours curled up in the bed reading. The Proper Thing to Do was to sit in the drawing room. And not loiter lawlessly in their chairs, either, as we did in ours when we thought she wasn't looking. But one felt no urge to loiter lawlessly in this drawing room, where I had seen no one sit but Mr Cephas.

Yet I was well into my book and transported far away; for now people were inside the house and I had not even heard them arrive. My father was showing me to a small party of men all more or less like him.

'That's the little scholar,' he was saying in a jaunty voice. 'See? Head in a book, *oui!* How you like that? This girl will be more scholar than the Prime Minister!'

I greeted the visitors and hurriedly got up to make myself scarce. But my father held me back. I had to shake the hand of each of his guests and stand uncomfortably by while they were told of how bright I was and what a large box of books ('a whole *library*, man') I had brought with me. Then I helped Miss Velma bring out glasses and ice before escaping to the bedroom.

The company settled down to drinking and chatting, and Mr Cephas put on music. I heard Miss Velma slip quietly into her bedroom. Out in the drawing room my father's voice was brimming over with jauntiness. Michael came in unnoticed through the back door and dived into his bed, covered from head to toe in the day's dust.

Miss Velma got up immediately and shuffled over to our room to tell us to come and eat.

While we were eating, Mr Cephas came to the kitchen door.

'Velma,' he said, 'fix up with some ice.'

Then his eyes focused on me: 'Eh-eh, doots, you finish reading? Come, man, come and give you daddy friends some ice. Let them see the scholar, man!'

Miss Velma gave me a bowl of ice and my father led me by the arm into the drawing room. He steered me from guest to guest for me to put ice in their glasses and for him to tell them again of my brains and my books and what a big-shot I was going to be when I grew up. He was very merry by this time.

We finished eating. Miss Velma persuaded Michael to take off his dirty clothes, but he drew the line at bathing. When the three of us went to sleep, the company was still loud and hearty in the drawing room.

The next morning Miss Velma and I cleared away the debris.

It was a very busy week. Miss Velma took me to the stores to get my books and school clothes. We bought yellow shirts and the yellow-and-brown plaid material for the skirts. Then we went from one shoe store to the next until we found good shoes at the right price.

When we had got everything I needed, Miss Velma counted up the money she had left, shut the purse, and winked at me. She took me back to the cloth store and we went home with material for three new dresses! When I thanked her, she said: 'Don't mind that, darling. Your Tantie Velma well glad she get a little girl to sew clothes for.'

During the week she took me to different parts of the town so that I would know my way around. I learned the way to the school and one day walked there and back by myself.

Miss Velma made my skirts and I tried on the whole uniform. It looked so smart! I wished that Ma and Pappy and Uncle Leroy and everybody at home could see me right away.

I spent hours with my new books. I began to read some of them. For this I needed peace and quiet and an orderly space around me. My belongings were still hidden under the bed and that was inconvenient. I couldn't play hide-and-seek with this little boy forever. I had to make myself comfortable.

I started by glaring at him whenever he came into the room making noise. I opened my eyes wide like a madwoman, bared my teeth, and rose up off the bed as if to spring on him.

He would look frightened and run out again.

Once he brought his mother. Poor Miss Velma stood in the doorway with him, puzzled, for he couldn't explain why he had dragged her there, and why he was so frantic. I raised my head from my book and smiled sweetly.

A little later he crept back. He lingered by the door and peeped in at me again and again. Finally, I called him in and he came, trying to put a swagger into his walk. I looked at him coldly.

'Now you just keep yourself quiet in here!' I hissed. He nodded. 'And if you bring your mother for me again,' I warned under my breath, for Miss Velma was about, 'I'll *pinch* you!'

Now he opened his eyes wide and looked ready to run out again. I grabbed him.

'You understand me?'

He was too frightened to answer.

'Answer me!'

'Yes,' he said meekly.

'"Yes," who?'

'Yes, Late ... Let ... Yes, I-don't-know!' He was desperate.

'Yes, Miss Laetitia Johnson,' I instructed, fighting to keep a straight face.

'Yes, Miss Lacytish ...' I couldn't help laughing.

That was exactly what had happened when Kenwyn first started to talk and tried to say my name, and that was where I had got my home name 'Lacey.'

'All right,' I said, patting Michael on a dirty cheek. 'Just say "Lacey," okay? Now' – I made my face stern again – 'make up that bed!'

'Make up ... the bed?' he asked in disbelief. He turned and tugged the sheet this way and that. The bed remained like a sea under hurricane. He picked up his cover from the floor and stood with it in his hand, showing me a pitiful face.

'How much years you have?' I asked.

'Nine.'

'Nine years! Nine years and you can't make up your bed? You ain't shame?'

He looked as if he was going to cry. I took one end of the cover and made him hold the other. Together we matched corner to corner and folded it. I made him shake and beat the pillow. I showed him how to pull the sheet taut and tuck it under the mattress. Then I instructed him to place the folded cover under the pillow.

'All right,' I said. 'What you going to do now?'

'Lie down,' he answered in a doubtful little voice, almost as a question.

'Eh-eh.' I shook my head. 'You too nasty to lie down on this bed. You have to go and bathe first.'

A shadow of protest passed over his face but quickly vanished. Then the corners of his mouth trembled downwards again and he left the room in haste. Whether he was going to the bathroom or to complain to his mother, I did not know. I settled back into the book I was reading.

I had quite forgotten Michael when later a little figure draped in a towel tiptoed into the room. There was soap in his hair and I felt a little guilty.

'You wash your hair, too! That is a nice boy. For that I'll read a story for you when you put on your clothes. You like stories?'

'Yes!' he breathed, and his face was one big eager smile as he dug for clothes in the rat nest that was his drawer.

On the first day of school the new students were collected together in the big hall again, where the principal first gave a little welcoming speech.

'And now,' she said, 'I'll hand you over to your form teachers. They will take you to your classrooms and chat with you for a bit. I know that today it will be the teachers doing all the chatting because you're not ready to open your mouths yet. But by next week I'll be hearing you from down in my office – I know!

'Listen carefully for your name. Each form teacher will call out the names of students in his or her form, girls first, and then boys. Each form is named after a flower, and carries the initial of that name:

> Form 1B for Balisier
> Form 1C for Chaconia
> Form 1F for Frangipani
> Form 1H for Hibiscus, and
> Form 1P for Poui

'One last thing: listen carefully. Your names will be called in alphabetical order, in pairs. You will line up, with your partner, and follow your teacher to your classroom. The person who is your partner today will be your partner for the week. You must stick together, help each other, look out for each other – for the rest of this week. If you don't like the person, too bad – you can't dump your partner until next week.'

Children giggled a little now, for already they were beginning to feel more relaxed.

I was placed in Form 1H and my partner was a girl named Anjanee Jugmohansingh. She came towards me smiling and looking straight into my face, as though she knew me and was glad to see me again.

'Morning, neighbour,' she said, and suddenly she did remind me of someone I knew: Charlene's mother, Tara.

I had not seen Tara for the longest while – not since Charlene was a baby. There was some commotion at her home before Charlene was born, and Ma brought Tara to stay with us 'until the old lady cool down and ready to take her back.' When Charlene was six months old, Tara got a job in the city, but her mother, Maharajin, would not let her take her baby with her.

Tara used to keep her hair short and bushy around her head, but this girl had two long plaits down to her waist and a donkey-mane almost falling into her eyes. She didn't look like Tara, but she reminded me of her because she seemed to be smiling not with happiness but with goodness of heart, a goodness that nothing could kill.

'Morning, neighb,' I answered Anjanee, and I couldn't help giving her a broad grin back.

We stood together in the line while the other

names were called, and then the whole line followed our little form teacher. She was so short that we couldn't see her as she walked at the front.

She took us first to our classroom and told us to sit anywhere we wanted. All the boys rushed to the back seats. Anjanee and I sat together in the fourth row.

Miss Hafeez introduced herself and then chatted with us for a while. Next she took us on a tour of the school and showed us where the toilets were, the locker area, the tuck-shop, the art room, the home-economics room, the woodwork room, and the music room. Then we went back to our class to talk about the school rules, our timetable, and other things that we needed to know about.

At break time Anjanee and I set out to find the toilet.

'This place big, eh?' I said, as we tried to figure out which way to turn. 'And suppose we get lost now and can't find back the classroom!'

We giggled at the thought, but getting lost in this maze did not seem so impossible. I would never have asked any of the self-important older students who were walking all around us and not paying us any mind; but Anjanee stopped a biggish girl and asked her the way. The girl directed us, looking at us with amusement, but Anjanee didn't seem to notice – she flashed the girl a bright smile and we went on.

At lunchtime most of the children were staying in the classroom to eat.

'Let's go and eat outside,' Anjanee whispered. She had taken a little brown paper parcel out of the desk

37

but was holding it on her lap. She seemed to be trying to hide it.

'Why we can't stay ...' I started to ask, but the pleading look on her face made me give in without any discussion.

We went down the stairs and along two or three corridors. Children were settling down in little bunches everywhere, taking out their food. Anjanee hurried past, keeping her parcel covered with an exercise book.

'Where we going, Anjanee? You know the way?'

'Let's go outside, na?'

I followed her patiently, for she seemed bent on getting as far away as possible from everybody. We went out on to the playing field and walked across to the far side, where the bush began. There we found a log to sit on, under a tree.

I was quite hungry by now, and I started to eat, but Anjanee hesitated to open her brown paper parcel. With a little half smile she said: 'Don't laugh at my lunch, you hear? Is not like what you have. Is only roti and talkarie.'

When she opened it, the Cephases' luncheon-meat sandwich turned tasteless in my mouth, and I became quite homesick. Anjanee's lunch smelled as good as the roti and talkarie that Uncle Leroy made for us!

'That is the best lunch, girl! Why you hiding it?'

She blushed and muttered something about 'town people.'

'Where you living?' I asked.

'Orangefield,' she said, trying to put a full stop to that topic.

'Well, I living Balatier. I only staying in town to go to school.'

She seemed very impressed, even a little envious, but didn't say anything.

'You staying home in Orangefield?' I asked, and she nodded.

'And travelling up every day?'

'Yes,' she said, and I wondered why she sounded so doubtful.

I sighed. 'I wish I could live home. I don't want to stay up here at all.'

'Who you staying by?' Anjanee asked.

'My father. But I going home every weekend. I ain't spending no weekend by he!'

The next morning Anjanee arrived very late – halfway through the geography class. She was embarrassed and flustered, as though coming to school late was the end of the world. I peered at her, but she kept her eyes straight ahead, looking at the teacher and, I thought, avoiding me.

After a while I realized that she had no geography book, so I put mine where she could see into it.

At break time she stayed in the classroom and put her head on the desk.

'What happen, Anjanee, you sick?' I asked.

'No,' she said. 'I just taking a little rest.'

She was trying to seem cheerful, but there was a terribly strained look on her face, as though all the cares of the world were weighing on her.

We had Spanish after the break, and again Anjanee had no book.

The teacher was a strange, flabby man with sagging cheeks who hid behind huge dark glasses and taught us by mumbling out of the Spanish book, which he held upright in front of him like a shield. It was clear from that first week that in his class we were not likely to learn very much and that sooner or later all hell would break loose.

Anjanee and I ate lunch again out on our log.

Before we could settle down, she said in a rush: 'I getting the rest of my books next week,' and started to eat with all her might. She looked so unhappy that I thought I would cheer her up by cracking jokes about the weird Spanish teacher, and the Circus-horse, Mrs Lopez.

She, it had turned out, was our maths teacher. The afternoon before, she had come into the classroom dressed to kill and taught us mathematics without noticing us.

'I don't know why that lady think she so nice,' I said. 'Her mother must be fool her.' (This Mammy Patsy used to say about people who gave themselves airs for no reason that anybody could see.) 'But the lady face just like a fowl bottom!'

Anjanee giggled, and chatted quite cheerfully for a while. Then the cloud came over her face again.

In maths that afternoon, Mrs Lopez gave us work to do out of the textbook. I shared mine with Anjanee, but she did not get much done because she could hardly hold her head up. She seemed to be fighting sleep all day long.

The rest of the afternoon was physical education, and Anjanee didn't have the P.E. uniform but still set out to run around the playing field with us. It was not long before she had to go and sit down in the shade of a tree.

There was heavy rain the next morning, and many children were late, among them Anjanee. We were over in the home-economics room, a big, pretty kitchen with shining bright sinks and stoves and tables, and a teacher like a mother hen. Mrs McAllister never sat down, and as she fluttered about from place to place, she kept saying: 'Now, *girls*, tidy, tidy as we go!' and: 'Into your groups, now, *girls!*' It was as if she couldn't see the five boys with us, large as life, who had chosen to do home ec instead of woodwork.

By lunchtime the rain had stopped, but it was too wet to eat outside, so Anjanee found us a new spot: a space behind the lockers where abandoned, broken furniture was stored. Students came to their lockers every now and then, so Anjanee never took her roti out of the paper bag. She would put the bag to her mouth and take a quick bite, close the bag and hold it on her lap again while she chewed.

When we had finished eating, we went back to the classroom, where many of our classmates were still eating lunch or simply playing around. The rain had kept everybody inside this lunch hour. Anjanee put her head down on the desk and, amid loud talking, laughter, and ruction, fell asleep.

On Thursday Anjanee did not come to school at all, and I had got so used to her that I went through the day feeling lost.

In social studies that afternoon we learned about Happy Families and their opposite, Broken Homes.

The teacher taught us that children who did not live in a house with their own exact mother and father were living in a Broken Home. Children living in such homes were Unhappy Children.

She stuck a large poster on to the blackboard. It was a colourful picture of some white people – a tall, square-jawed man looking ahead of him with great determination; a little woman with yellow hair who didn't quite come up to the man's shoulder; and next to the woman a boy and a girl with round, red cheeks, the boy up to the woman's waist, the girl up to the boy's shoulder. They looked like a staircase. All four were holding hands, and except for the man, who looked square-jawed and determined, they seemed very pleased about something that was not in the picture.

When she had got the poster up firmly – it kept slipping, and fell to the floor a few times, for the tape wouldn't hold – she told us to study it, and then draw in our notebooks a Happy Family.

To the right and left of me, children were obediently drawing square-jawed men, women with flowing yellow hair, and children with cheeks like apples, neatly ranged in staircase order. The teacher was walking around complimenting them on their work.

Then she was standing over me. Spread over two pages of my notebook were: Ma, Pappy, Uncle Leroy, Mammy Patsy, Uncle Jamesie, Tantie Monica, me, my sister, my brother, Carlyle, and all my first cousins. I was still working on the last of Uncle Jamesie's children, the baby, when the teacher made a little sound of annoyance.

'Where are the husband and wife?' she asked, frowning.

To get rid of her, I pointed out Ma and Pappy.

It didn't work. 'And they have *all* those children!' she exclaimed in mock alarm.

I didn't think it worth my while explaining anything to this woman, so I just sat and waited patiently for her to move on.

'Now, think about it,' she nagged, '*can* that family be happy? No, I don't think so. That looks like the family of the Old Woman Who Lived in a Shoe!'

Not all of our teachers were foolish people, though. We did have some sensible ones. There was Miss Hafeez, our form teacher, who also taught us science; and there was the man who had rescued the Circushorse from Ma on registration day. His name was Mr Joseph, and he was our English teacher.

In our first literature class, Mr Joseph told us that there was one book on our booklist that we could safely leave at home for the time being, and that was *Tales of the Greek Heroes*. We would read that book later, after we had written our own book.

He said that *Tales of the Greek Heroes* was a book of old-time folktales like our Anansi stories. These were just somebody else's 'Nansi stories – they came from Greece, which was on the other side of the world.

First we had to make a list of the 'Nansi stories we would write. He called for suggestions, but nobody was willing to say anything.

'Come on, you don't know any of your own folktales?' he coaxed the class. 'Eh? Nobody ever heard of the Ladjablesse?'

At this there was a loud burst of laughter. Children put their hands over their mouths, snickering, whispering and peeping at each other in embarrassment. Mr Joseph stood looking at us patiently, and, I thought, sadly.

Then a boy stood up and said in a brave voice: 'Yes, sir, I know – Papa Bois, Douenn ...' Children shrieked with laughter again, but Mr Joseph turned and solemnly wrote on the board the names of all these beings whom we knew, yes, but what would they be doing up here in our high-school literature class? The Ladjablesse, the Soucouyant, Anansi ... This moonlight world of people who were half beast, half spirit or half god, obviously only made up by our big-people to frighten us – Mr Joseph was insisting on writing their names up on the board!

The giggling died down as the class realized that he was quite serious.

Suddenly he turned and opened his *Tales of the*

Greek Heroes and started to read. The part he chose was from the story of the Cyclops, who was three times the size of an ordinary human being, had one big eye in the centre of his forehead, and ate two Greeks for breakfast.

Mr Joseph stopped reading and looked at us. The class was quiet and attentive.

'Eh-eh!' Mr Joseph exclaimed. 'You forget to laugh! You don't find this Cyclops fella jokey? Picture him, na! One big eye in the centre of his forehead! Eating two fellas for breakfast! He not as jokey as the Ladjablesse with her one good foot and one cow foot, leading foolish men astray in the bush? Or Anansi the scheming spiderman? Eh-eh. The Cyclops not funny like them?'

On Friday morning I got up very early. I was going home for the weekend! My bag was already packed, from the night before, and I would take it to school with me. It was the little travelling bag that Mammy Patsy had sent from New York since last Christmas. The bag was still brand-new and smelled of mothballs, because Ma had kept it hidden away somewhere, in case she or any one of us ever had to go to the hospital.

After school I would head straight for the bus station. I couldn't wait!

I was very excited, and happier still to see Anjanee again.

'What happen to you yesterday?' I asked her.

'I ... I miss the bus,' she answered. I could sense that there was more to it than that, but she wasn't going to tell me. In any case, I was so glad to be going home that I couldn't think of much else.

At the end of the day we walked to the bus station together. I was almost skipping down the road, until I noticed that Anjanee was walking with a heavy step, and that while I had been chattering all the way, she only answered now and then in a small, dull voice.

'What happen?' I asked. 'You feeling sick?'

She flashed me a glance and shook her head, and we walked on in silence to the bus station. There we found a place to sit and wait. Buses were revving up their engines and schoolchildren skylarking all around us, but there were many people talking to each other quietly, under the din.

I was determined to find out what was wrong with my friend.

'You don't like the school?'

'Yes, I like the school – I want to go to school,' she answered quickly. 'But I don't know if ... I don't know how I will get to go.'

'Because you living so far?'

Orangefield, I knew, was another village placed like Sooklal Trace – far from the main road. But they were even worse off, because there were no buses at all running near them. If her family didn't have money for the taxi to Caigual, where she could catch the bus, then this girl was really in trouble.

'You don't have nobody here in town you could stay by?'

She opened her eyes wide with alarm. 'You mad! They don't even want me to come out of the house! They want me to stay in the house!'

Then she began to speak slowly, quietly, as if to herself. 'My big brothers and my father ... they saying that I go to school enough already, that I know how to read and write, and cook and wash, so what I harassing them for with booklist and uniform and taxi fare ...'

She was overcome. Her eyes filled up with tears

and she stared straight ahead. We sat in a helpless silence until it was time for her to go.

A little later I got on to my bus, with a heavy heart now. It was two weeks since I had left home. I couldn't wait to see everybody again – Ma and the little children, Uncle Leroy, Pappy ... but I knew that Anjanee would be on my mind all weekend.

My spirits began to lift as the bus picked up speed and the world outside grew greener and greener. When we reached Junction I got off and waited at the bus station among a growing crowd of County Council workers, schoolchildren who had stayed late for Common Entrance lessons, people who had come to sell in the market or to buy goods in the store ... The Balatier bus left Junction full to bursting, as usual, and it seemed to stop and let off people at every shop, every corner, every lamppost along the road.

By the time I got off at Rampie's corner and started walking in, evening was coming down on the Trace. Children were bringing in goats and cows. There was woodsmoke in the air – people were roasting bakes or warming talkarie. I was looking forward to getting my teeth into a good heavy piece of roast bake. Already I was tired of the soft, neatly sliced bread that Miss Velma bought in the grocery: it felt like cottonwool in your mouth.

I called out greetings to houses along the way, feeling proud when people looked out and saw me in my uniform.

When I reached our gap, I could see Ruth and Kenwyn sitting on the front steps, waiting. It was already a little dark and they didn't see me until I was almost halfway up the path. First they rushed down the steps towards me, but then they turned back and ran inside, shouting: 'Ma! Ma! She come! She come!' Then they flew out again, but halfway down the steps they stopped in their tracks, overcome with shyness.

By now the dogs were roused, and they shot out from under the house, barking, yelping, whining, jostling with each other. They flung their bodies against my legs, they jumped up and tried to lick my face, they lay on their backs with their four legs in the air and wriggled.

Uncle Leroy appeared from nowhere and took the travelling bag and my schoolbag, shooing the dogs away, while Ma stood at the front door and just beamed.

We were up until very late. I had to tell them everything I could remember about the school and about the Cephases. Uncle Leroy said that he would have to come and see this Circus-horse for himself one day, and that he and Pappy would have to teach me the little bush Spanish that they knew, if this Mr Tewarie wasn't teaching me anything. Michael he suggested I bring home for one weekend for Ma to straighten out.

Every now and then my grandmother asked: 'And how your father and he wife treating you, eh?'

'They treating me okay, Ma,' was all I could say, for I couldn't complain that they weren't. Yet Ma could tell that I was not overjoyed to be living there, so she kept coming back to the Cephases.

Finally she sent us off to our beds.

The next morning I woke up early to go and look at my garden, the fowls, the pigs, the plum tree. Later, after I had done my homework, I went down to the big garden with Uncle Leroy and Carlyle. Uncle Leroy said I was more use than Carlyle, who thought that weekends were for putting on a pretty jersey and stepping out to Junction to watch kung-fu pictures.

Carlyle tried to stifle the grin that leapt to his face, and he began to work more furiously. There was a kung-fu double on at the Odeon that afternoon and he was hoping that Uncle Leroy would let him go.

'You see how he smiling?' said Uncle Leroy. 'I think this boy have girlfriend in Junction and all.'

Carlyle became quite flustered, and when he opened his mouth to protest; his voice came out in a croak, as it often did of late.

Uncle Jamesie, Tantie Monica, and my cousins came up on Sunday. Uncle Jamesie brought his camera and I had to put on my school uniform and pose with my bookbag so that he could take some pictures of me to send for my mother.

I was getting ready to leave with Uncle Jamesie on Sunday afternoon, and as the time drew closer I must have started to look very miserable, for Ma called me into her room and shut the door. I was sorry to be leaving, yes, but a worried feeling had come over me, too, when I thought of Anjanee.

'How your father treating you?' she asked anxiously, peering into my face. 'He hit you? That man hit you? Tell me, you know, tell me if that man raise his hand for you, because you know your Uncle

Leroy would go down there now for now and break his backside! That man like to hit – we know he like to hit!'

She questioned me and coaxed me until I seemed to brighten up.

Anjanee didn't talk about herself any more. It was as though she felt that she had said too much already. Now she was reluctant even to share my textbooks in class, and kept saying that she was getting her own books 'next week'.

One day her pen spattered and we both got ink on our shirts. By the end of a fortnight I realized that Anjanee had only one shirt, for every day I saw the same pattern of ink dots on her sleeve.

Then she disappeared for three days. When she came back to school she was tight-lipped. She wouldn't breathe a word about why she had missed three whole days in a row.

We were sitting on our log, far away across the playing field, eating lunch. I was questioning her, trying to find out what had happened, and she stubbornly refused to talk.

I lost my patience and got up from the log.

'Well, we can't be friends,' I reproached her, 'if we going to keep secrets from one another.'

Anjanee dropped her face into her hands and began to cry. I sat down again and tried to eat my words. 'I only making joke, Anjanee. You don't have to tell me.'

Then, after a pause, during which she kept her face buried in her hands, I added: 'I know it was because you didn't have money. But I don't see why you shame for that. We ain't have no money neither, and I ain't shame.'

Slowly she lifted her head out of her hands and straightened her shoulders. She began to talk.

On the Monday morning she had gone to each brother in turn, and then her father, for money to pay the taxi fare. Her mother had been squeezing money out of what they gave her every week to go to the shop, and giving it to Anjanee to pay the taxi to Caigual. But that week there wasn't a cent left over. Her brothers and her father had each brushed her off, saying they had no money. Then she had started over again, going back to her biggest brother, the one who had a regular job with the County Council.

He made a terrible scene. He told her he would break her foot if that was the only way to make her stay home and do her work. She was out of the house all day, going out early, early in the morning and reaching home near night-time, leaving her mother to do all the work. Why should he waste his good money sending her to any *high school*, for she was high enough already and in fact a little too high with herself. She was a girl and already knew everything a girl needed to know. Why would she want to know more than her mother?

When her father and one brother set out for the garden, and the two other brothers went to work, Anjanee and her mother picked some vegetables from her mother's kitchen garden, and Anjanee went round the village with a tray on her head selling what she could.

She did this for two days, and on the third day was flat in bed with fever and a headache from having walked about in the sun for hours.

Now she stopped talking and we both sat and stared across the field. What was to be done?

'I don't want to end up like my mother!' Anjanee said vehemently. 'I *not* going to end up like my mother, I rather dead. If you see how much work my mother does have to do when the day come! And only me to help her. After me is only little children. So only me to get up four o'clock in the morning and help her knead the flour so everybody could eat and get food to carry. Only me to help her bring water and bathe the little ones for school, feed the baby, wash everybody clothes, iron everybody clothes, sweep the house, sweep the yard, cook a ton load of food in the evening again ... And they don't even *see* her, you know that? They don't even *know how much work she doing. And she working day and night for them* – she don't get to do one thing for herself. They does just come home and eat, mess up the house, drop their dirty clothes ... If it was me I would just walk away one day and leave them there in their mess. But when I tell her so, she does just shake her head and say "Where I will leave them and go, *beti*? I ain't have schooling. You want me go by the side of the road and beg?"'

Michael was trying very hard not to annoy me. He made sure to keep me in a good mood so that I would read stories to him. When I came into the room now, I always found it looking neat. But sometimes this meant that his cover was gathered into a heap and stuffed under his pillow, or that hiding under the bed was a mess of shoes, guns, clothes, cars, and marbles. Still, I only had to raise my eyebrows to get him to finish the job.

He didn't spend much time at home. Every day he would come home from school and drop his bookbag in the drawing room. Then he would go into the kitchen and lift the cover off every pot and peer inside. If he liked the food, he would stay and eat some. If it was something he didn't like, he would leave immediately, sometimes not even bothering to take off his school uniform.

Miss Velma fretted and fretted. She begged him to do his homework, to eat some food, to bathe, to come home early. And Mr Cephas, when he was at home and not polishing his car, sat in the drawing room and Took His Son in Hand.

'Michael! Take your book and come here!' he'd call out in a voice like a policeman.

Michael would look dismayed and spend as long as possible searching for his reading book, which usually meant that his father had to summon him again, this time with threats. Then he would find the book and walk with fear and trembling towards the chair where Mr Cephas sat.

The reading lesson always ended badly. For Michael couldn't read to save his life. He would guess and mumble his way through every sentence, and Mr Cephas would get more and more exasperated, and bellow at him, and clap him behind the head every time he got a word wrong, and finally batter him with the book.

'Where I get this blockhead?' he would rage. 'Where? Man, this child going to make me shame! What going to become of you, boy? You want to be a cane cutter? Eh? You want to cut cane or make garden for your living? Eh?'

'No, Daddy,' came a meek voice.

'Well, why you don't learn your lesson, boy, you want to make me shame? You want to be a good-for-nothing?'

Sometimes Mr Cephas would work up such a rage that he took off his belt and started to beat Michael. At this Miss Velma would come out from wherever she had hidden herself, and plead with Mr Cephas to spare him.

'Spare him? Spare him so he could be a damn good-for-nothing? Is you that spoiling him, you know, is you that turning him into a damn good-for-nothing!' And he shook the belt in her face.

Miss Velma would haul Michael to safety, and he would hide in the bedroom, still trembling, until his father went to bed or left the house.

Mr Cephas also took a great deal of interest in my schoolwork – a little too much for my liking. When he saw me at the table with my books, he would hover over me, looking, as my mother would say, like the cat that got the canary. Sometimes he would sit in the drawing room and go through my schoolbooks, every now and then smacking his lips or giving out a foolish little chuckle.

Miss Velma I still could not figure out. She crept about her own house as though she were frightened. I never saw her sit in the drawing room, and she only sat at the dining-room table for Sunday lunch. She always spoke in a low, apologizing voice, especially when Mr Cephas was at home. When he was not there she seemed anxious, and spent hours in the gallery like a dog waiting for its owner. But when he was at home it was as though she were hiding in corners and shadows.

I wondered whether she had any friends, or family, for I never saw anybody visit her. On the day I went to church with her, she had joined a circle of her church sisters after the service. She stood chatting quite gaily with them until she looked at her watch and very abruptly left them.

Ma said that Mr Cephas was one of those foolish people who believed that white people sat at the right hand of God and black people under His chair, and that the next best thing to being white was to marry somebody white or whitish. So he had married a red-skinned woman to show how he was moving up in the world. But that didn't make a great deal of sense to me. There was nothing *up* about Miss Velma. Looking at her, you would think, instead, that there was something pressing her *down*, pressing down her whole life, like a plant in too much shade that couldn't thrive.

At home on weekends I tended my garden, and there was always something new – a hard, round baby pumpkin the size of a marble; yellow-and-maroon flowers brightening the pigeon-pea trees; a bunch of baby bananas that seemed to have sprouted out of nowhere.

These weekends were much too short. Ma made me leave for La Puerta on the Sunday afternoon. I wanted to stay and take the bus to school on Monday mornings, but she would not hear of it.

One Friday there was a letter from my mother waiting for me. She wanted to know about my school, whether my father had bought my books and my uniform, and whether I was still comfortable in his house.

Now that your father is helping you and the government is giving you your secondary education, I can try to do something for myself. I enrolled in night classes for the High School Diploma. So you see, the two of us are going to secondary school together. But it is hard, hard, hard. After I finish work at the hospital, sometimes five, sometimes six o'clock, I eat a sandwich (sometimes I don't even have time for that) and I run to the subway to get the train. When I reach the school I am tired, tired. Sometimes I fall asleep in class. Sometimes I think I am too old to learn, that my brain is seized up, for I don't understand everything. One of the teachers is a lady from Antigua, and she takes pity on me and helps me with what I don't understand. It is hard, but I will fight up with it as long as I know that you all are okay. Tell Pappy he brought me luck. I wrote an essay about him and it got an A. We had to write about 'A person who has inspired you.'

Give everybody a kiss for me.

Whenever we heard from Mammy Patsy, my grandmother would sit holding the letter for a long time, talking to herself. Off and on she would smile, and then sigh, and then smile proudly again.

That evening she muttered about how since Patsy had gone, and now Lacey, she had no Chief Cook and Bottle-Washer.

It was now almost two years since Mammy Patsy had left for New York. She used to work in the garden and in the cocoa with Ma and Uncle Leroy. Pappy helped, too, whenever his back would permit, but they didn't let him do too much of the heavy work like cutlassing or digging drains.

My mother also used to help Ma with the sugar-cake and other things we made to sell.

All the children would be sent out into the land to gather coconuts, and Ma and Mammy Patsy husked them with the cutlass. Carlyle and I helped to grate them.

Only the big-people could stir the pot of boiling coconut and sugar and spice on the fireside. They wouldn't let us come near the pot because, they said, the coconut could pitch up and burn a hole in your skin. When it was almost ready, I had to lay out the fig leaves on which Ma dropped the little blobs of sugar-cake. I was in charge of brushing away flies until the sugar-cakes were hard enough to be covered with a cloth. Later we packed them into the big biscuit tins.

When *pommes-cythères* were green but full, we peeled them and set them in salt water with seasoning. I helped to shell tamarinds for the tamarind balls.

Ma and Mammy Patsy used to go and sell all these things at the bus station in Junction on Saturday mornings and sometimes in the week. After my mother went away, Ma started taking Carlyle with her to help, but if Uncle Leroy needed Carlyle in the garden, I would go with Ma.

Now that I was away at school and could not help Ma during the week, I wanted to go to Junction with her on Saturdays.

'Let me come with you, Ma?' I'd ask as she was turning around in the kitchen, getting her things ready.

'No, madam. They ain't give you no homework to do? Well, you stay and do it. Give those little ones their tea, and then sit down with your book. Where this Carlyle? *Carlyle!* Look, go and call that boy before he and me fall out this early morning!'

Carlyle was finished with school, but what was to become of him Ma said she did not know. Though he had warmed the bench in post-primary class for two years, she wasn't sure that he could read A, B, or C, or sign his own name.

Form 1H was beginning to show its colours. There began to be little clashes with teachers, and some students were already trying out the school rules that in our first week we had pledged to obey.

Now, everybody knew, but nobody would breathe a word, that Doreen Sandiford and her gang had been to the Plaza at least twice, to buy chicken and chips. The La Puerta Shopping Plaza was most strictly out of bounds, and to break this rule was a Very Serious Offence, for which students would be suspended. We were banned from the Plaza, Miss Hafeez had explained, because there had been cases of students shoplifting, and because there were drug pushers in the Plaza whose speciality was schoolchildren.

Nobody dared to tell on Doreen Sandiford and her gang. We wouldn't dream of it. Doreen Sandiford was a tall, strapping girl with a hoarse voice who looked as though she could mash a man into the ground.

Even Marlon Peters had respect for Doreen Sandiford. He was the ringleader of a gang of boys who had taken on the job of keeping things lively in class. Marlon Peters's gang 'fell' off their chairs on cue, they dropped the pans that contained their maths instruments on to the floor, they farted. But it all depended on who the teacher was. They tried none of that on Miss Hafeez nor on Mr Joseph.

In literature class Mr Joseph was reading a book to us, a chapter at a time. It was called *The Year in San Fernando*, and it was the only thing that could make Marlon Peters and his gang pay attention. In fact, whenever it was time for *The Year in San Fernando*, Marlon Peters and Naushad Ali would pick up their chairs and move to the front of the class. There they sat, as still as statues, listening. If anyone made the slightest noise, the two of them would turn and glare at that person.

But nobody would wilfully disturb Mr Joseph when he was reading this story. The whole class was captivated. It was a story about *us*, and *our* world! We were surprised, and thrilled, that the ordinary, everyday things we took part in could find their way into a story! It meant that we were real, and had weight, like the people in stories. As important as we felt in Mr Joseph's class, though, Mrs Lopez was always there to turn us into nothing.

She would float into the classroom on a cloud of elegant perfume, teach her maths scornfully, and depart again with her head still in the air. Whether or not we understood anything was no concern of hers. We didn't often ask questions, either. Nobody wanted to disturb her. We were not good enough.

One day Anjanee put God out of her thoughts and asked Mrs Lopez to explain something.

The Circus-horse pretended first of all that she could not find the owner of the voice. She stopped in her tracks, narrowed her eyes, and searched all over the classroom.

Anjanee put up her hand again.

'Yes?' said the Circus-horse in an icy voice.

Anjanee asked the question once more, trembling now.

'Try paying attention in class!' Mrs Lopez snapped, and in the same voice threw her a rapid answer to the question. It was more of a scolding than an explanation.

'Don't bother with she,' I said to Anjanee. 'I will show you.'

The Circus-horse finished off her lesson and then gave us exercises to work on. She sat marking papers.

I drew closer to Anjanee and began to explain to her what she did not understand.

The voice of the Circus-horse cut in: 'You two over there! Stop talking in my class!'

'I explaining the maths to Anjanee,' I said, and not in my most respectful voice.

'You "explaining the maths to Anjanee"? You are the teacher now? You taking over my job?'

The class sat up. The usual low rumble was starting to form. We had never gone further than that with Mrs Lopez – everybody would murmur and protest under their breath, but nobody would actually say anything for her to hear.

'Well, she ask you to explain it and she still don't understand,' I said in an accusing voice.

A new buzz of excitement rose from the class. By now Doreen Sandiford had begun to suck her teeth loudly behind her hand, and others were chattering heatedly, but still under their breath. Nobody wanted to be singled out, for this woman made people feel like cockroaches. Circus-horse looked thunderstruck for a moment, and then took charge once more.

'Madam, don't bring your rudeness here for me, you hear? Leave that at home!'

'I didn't say anything rude.' There was war in my voice, and I was looking straight into her face in the way I knew a child should not look at an adult. Yet for some reason she did not march me off to the principal's office. Instead, she drew herself up to her full height and began to give a lecture to the whole class. She seemed grateful for the opportunity.

You can take people out of the gutter, she informed us, but you can't take the gutter out of people. You can take a pig out of a pigsty, but you can't take the pigsty out of the pig. Some of us insisted on showing up by our behaviour the kind of *hole* we came out of. She had to say *hole* and not *home* because people who came out of proper *homes* knew how to behave. The government was wasting taxpayers' money sending us to secondary school, because we were not going to turn out any different from our parents. Here she gave a *Hmph!*

'Parents? Some of you don't even *have* parents – mother here, father there – and the government sending you to *secondary school*, if you please, to give decent people a hard time, casting pearls before swine …'

I could have told her that I, for one, was glad that my father was nowhere near my mother, but she wouldn't have heard. She had so much to say that it was only the bell that stopped her.

The Circus-horse gathered up her books and papers and stalked out, leaving us in a tense silence. Into this silence full of danger walked poor Mr Tewarie.

For the first few moments we completely ignored him. The class sat quietly boiling with vexation at the Circus-horse and at ourselves. Then we flew into a rage and all started talking at the same time. Mr Tewarie stood nervously by as our noise grew louder and hands waved angrily in the air. We would do for that witch. We would do for her. We would put a thumbtack on her chair, push her down the stairs, scrape her car, go to the principal, write to the government, complain to our parents.

Mr Tewarie began to make a feeble protest. Nobody paid him any mind. But he was getting angrier and angrier, until all meekness left him and he shocked us by suddenly slamming his book on to the table. The class fell silent; it was our turn to be nervous.

'What the hell is going on here! This is a fish market or what! You can't behave yourselves, you damn jokers, you can't behave? Take out your Spanish books!'

The class stayed quiet, and in the few minutes of peace we learned to say 'Mother is making an omelette.'

Then you began to hear little muffled sounds of

commotion coming from different parts of the class-room. A noise was building up again.

Suddenly a girl ran screaming from her seat and took refuge behind Mr Tewarie. He was very startled.

'What is this? What the hell is going on here? What happen to you, child? Who trouble you?'

It was foolish Joanne Carr, prim and proper and afraid of her own shadow. Teasing her was one of the favourite occupations of the boys in the class.

'Sir, they put something on me, sir,' she wailed.

Mr Tewarie turned automatically towards Marlon Peters. At that moment a member of Marlon Peters's gang sitting near me slipped a matchbox on to my desk and sat back straining to look innocent. I peered into the box. There lay nothing but a dead cockroach.

The class was in uproar again. Mr Tewarie was shouting at Marlon Peters and everyone was holding a loud, excited discussion with a neighbour. I took up the cockroach by its feelers and walked to the teacher's table, to present it to Mr Tewarie. But he was too busy with Marlon Peters and did not see me. I put the cockroach on the table. When Joanne Carr caught sight of it, she started screaming again. Then Mr Tewarie turned and saw the cockroach, too, and nearly jumped out of his skin ...

Choking with anger, Mr Tewarie sent out Marlon Peters, Wayne Joseph, and Anderson Lewis. Marlon Peters protested: 'Sir, what about Persad and Ali, sir? Them was in it, too!' A chorus of voices agreed. It seemed to us that Mr Tewarie was always letting off the Indian boys in the gang, and blaming Peters and the rest for everything.

'Get out of here! Get out of here before I go for the principal!' Mr Tewarie roared.

Lewis and Joseph grabbed each other and rushed out of the door with wide-open eyes and funny, jerky movements, like cartoon characters. Marlon Peters sauntered out, singing under his breath:

> Coolie, coolie
> Come for roti
> All the roti done.

Mr Tewarie, in shock, summoned him back.

'Yes, sir? Me, sir?' Marlon Peters stuck his head through the door, with a stupid grin spread across his face.

'What is that! What kind of thing is that I hear you singing? Right in front of me? Eh?' Mr Tewarie was going to burst. 'Damn jokers! That is what you fellas are! A damn set of jokers, man! Damn baboons! Damn good-for-nothing baboons!'

Marlon Peters came back into the classroom, still grinning: 'Sir, that is a song I hear the other day, sir. You want me to sing it for you, sir?'

And he sang the other verse:

> Nigger is a nation
> Damn botheration
> Gi' them a kick
> And send them in the station.

And he did an Indian dance all the way to the door, rocking his head on his neck and twirling his hands in front of him.

Children shrieked, booed, laughed, sang along with him, beat their rulers on their geometry pans, danced in the aisles ... And really, we had nothing much against poor Mr Tewarie.

Michael was a new little boy. He was folding his cover neatly every day, and putting his toys away, and even bathing without being asked. I continued to read to him, sometimes a whole story, sometimes part of a story. I often stopped at the most exciting point and left him battling to find out the rest for himself. Sometimes he finished the story by asking me every other word. Sometimes he struggled so pitifully with the words – his forehead squeezed into a knot and shoulders hunched over the book – that I gave in and finished it for him.

But he got better and better at it. He began to tackle books on his own. Now I could bribe him to sweep the room by bringing home books for him from the school library. He learned to sweep quite clean – even Ma would have been satisfied.

One evening I was teaching him to wash dishes. Miss Velma was at her post in the gallery with the *Daily Word*, for Mr Cephas was out. I was giving instructions to Michael, and Michael was talking without stopping, like a parrot. Now that he was no longer afraid of me, he could not stop chattering. He would talk for hours if I didn't shut him up.

Michael was standing on a stool at the sink –

splashing water, playing with the soap, and talking his head off. Mr Cephas was suddenly upon us.

He gasped and rushed back out towards the gallery. Michael fell silent. He stopped playing in the sink and started to wash dishes in earnest, thinking, perhaps, that his father would be pleased at his helpfulness.

Mr Cephas was ranting in the drawing room and the angry sound was coming closer. Then he was in the kitchen again, with Miss Velma meek and cowering behind him. She was looking as if he had dragged her bodily through the house.

'Washing wares! Washing wares!' Mr Cephas was shouting at her. 'In the kitchen, *washing wares!* I tired talk to you about how you turning this boy into a damn *cunumunu*! No wonder he can't learn his book! Two female in the house and my son have to be washing wares! Boy, get your tail down from there! And if your mother put you to wash wares again, tell her to go to hell!'

And twice his hand flew up as if to hit Miss Velma, and she cringed each time.

I was opening my mouth to say to Mr Cephas that it was not Miss Velma ... but Miss Velma shot me a glance which said I should be quiet.

She was right. Mr Cephas knew full well that she had not made Michael wash the dishes. Miss Velma couldn't make Michael do anything. So Mr Cephas must have known that I was the one who had him over the sink. But throughout his ranting he never once looked in my direction.

Later in the evening he called Michael, in a grim voice, to come and read. Although Michael could read much better now, he still baulked and stalled when his father ordered him to read (and the school reading book contained so much foolishness that anybody would choke on it). That evening Mr Cephas beat him with the reading book, his belt, his slipper, and a carved walking stick that was part of the drawing-room decorations. Miss Velma stayed hidden.

The following afternoon Miss Velma called me into her bedroom. There was a photograph album on the bed, and this she invited me to look through.

It began with pictures of herself as a young girl, posing in gardens and on steps with her skirt gaily spread out around her, pictures of her taken in studios, against painted walls of sea, mountain, or flowery meadow. In one photograph she was wearing a school uniform. In all, she was a laughing, lively young person.

There was her wedding picture, with Mr Cephas looking like a fattened penguin in his three-piece suit, and Miss Velma with life still shining out from her. There were pictures of Michael, an ugly baby, bald and with an old man's face.

While I looked through the album, Miss Velma was sorting the clothes that she had just taken off the line. Suddenly she said: 'You mustn't go against them, you know. Your father, you mustn't go against him. It don't pay to get them vex. When you get big and you have your husband, you will know for yourself. Jump high or jump low, you have to please them. That is a woman's lot.'

She took the album and turned back to the picture of herself in school uniform. In the picture she looked about twelve years old.

'I was a bright little girl like you, you know. Bright as a bulb, they used to say. I start to go to secondary school, too. But it wasn't like now. In those days you had to pay school fees. And then they only had secondary schools in the city. So when you add up school fees, bus fare, books, uniform, lunch ... Well – when my younger brother reach the age for secondary school, they take me out and put him in. They didn't have the money to pay for two. And it's more important for a boy to get education. They put me by a lady to learn sewing. Then I went to work in a shirt factory. When I meet your father, I was working there. As soon as we get married, he make me leave the job.'

Miss Velma sighed and her talkative mood vanished. There was still a mountain of clothes on the bed to be sorted out before the hours of ironing began – mostly Michael's and Mr Cephas's shirts, jerseys, vests, trousers, shorts, underpants, socks, towels, washcloths, handkerchiefs ... I made a move to help her, but she waved me away: 'No, child. That is *my* work. You take your book and study your lesson. And study it *good*.'

There was nobody in our class who did not feel for Anjanee. Although I was the only one who really knew her, the others could tell that all was not well with their classmate. They sympathized with Anjanee and they liked her because she was so warm and good-natured.

The children in the class were always trying to help Anjanee – offering to share their textbooks with her, giving her copybook pages when hers ran out, prompting her under their breath when a teacher asked her a question that she could not answer. One day in P.E. Anjanee felt faint and had to sit down in the middle of the field. Before the teacher could say anything, a whole band of children, led by Marlon Peters and Naushad Ali, was racing desperately towards the home-ec room to get a glass of water for her.

Now everyone was quietly up in arms against the Circus-horse for the way that she was treating Anjanee. There was no love lost between Mrs Lopez and any of us, but Anjanee had become her special scapegoat.

A good half of the class was no better at maths than Anjanee. Marlon Peters and Wayne Joseph were utterly hopeless at it and furthermore did not care a damn.

But Anjanee tried, and worried, and put out every ounce of effort she could squeeze from her tired body. She did her homework in the lunch hour, when she could use my book. In class she did not let anything distract her – she listened intently to every word that fell out of the Circus-horse's mouth, rubbing her eyes to chase away sleep. Sometimes her head fell forward suddenly on to her chest but immediately shot up again. Then she sat bolt upright, looking around her in confusion. On some days she simply had to put her head down on the desk for a few seconds at a time. But always she would rouse herself and bravely tackle whatever work we were given in class.

Yet Circus-horse was always throwing her most sarcastic remarks at Anjanee. She referred to her as 'Miss Jugmohansingh,' with a sneer in her voice. Some people in the class were hardly ever called upon to answer questions, but Circus-horse never forgot to spring them on Anjanee. She asked Anjanee questions which she knew full well she couldn't answer, and insulted her when the girl either gave the wrong answer or just stared speechlessly, at a loss.

Mrs Lopez wrote all over Anjanee's exercise books with her hurtful red-ink pen: 'Hopeless.' 'You will never learn.' 'This is *disgraceful*. You haven't a clue and you never will.' And so on.

Anjanee came to school one Monday and disappeared for the rest of the week. I grew more despondent every day that she didn't turn up, afraid that Anjanee had dropped out now for good. Of late she had begun to talk about giving up the struggle.

But if Anjanee ever had to drop out of school she would slowly shrivel up and die. She was so determined not to end up like her mother! Anjanee wanted to pass her exams and get a job and a place to live, and take her mother to live with her. Anjanee would cook and clean for the two of them. Her mother would never have to lift a finger again – she would just wear nice clothes, and get fat and healthy, and go to the cinema every weekend to see love movies, Indian and English.

I was miserable, and frightened. Every morning I hoped that Anjanee would scurry into the classroom in the way that she always did, trying to make herself invisible because she was so late.

Anybody would think that the Circus-horse also missed her sorely, for again and again she inquired after 'Miss Jugmohansingh.'

On Friday, at the beginning of the maths period, she looked around the classroom for Anjanee and remarked: 'So Miss Jugmohansingh has left us?' Then she turned to clean the blackboard, adding not quite under her breath: 'That is one less dunce. One less headache for me. Praise God.'

This was too much for the class. Immediately the grumbling started up. I was so angry that I couldn't talk. Anjanee might be sick or dying, for all this woman knew. And if Anjanee had, in fact, given up, then this woman had helped to drive her out of school.

I made a loud noise with my chair to catch Mrs

Lopez's attention, and then, looking her straight in the eye, I pushed my pan of maths instruments off the desk.

A few seconds of silence passed. Then a little mousy girl sitting near me – a girl who was so quiet and unnoticeable that my mother would have named her God-Rest-the-Dead – positioned her pan at the front of her desk and with a wide movement of her whole arm swept it over the edge.

Then, all over the classroom, pans crashed to the floor, spilling out compasses, set squares, pencils, rulers ... The noise was deafening.

Circus-horse had no words for this occasion. 'I am going for the principal' was all she said, as she gathered her belongings and shot through the door.

We waited for the principal. Doreen Sandiford was the lookout. She stood in the doorway, ready to dart back into her seat at the first glimpse of the principal. The rest of us held a noisy conference to decide what we would tell her. Our books were open before us so that when Doreen gave the signal we would stop talking and start to 'study' with all our might.

But the principal never came. As the days went by, we got used to the Circus-horse marching out of the classroom to 'go for the principal'.

Mr Tewarie never bothered to threaten us with any principal. After two or three more scuffles with our class, he just went straight to Miss Hafeez and told on us.

She walked into the classroom one morning with irritation on her face. 'Okay, 1H, so why will you not behave in your Spanish class?'

She put down the register and stood looking at us, waiting for an answer. We stared back at her with over-innocent faces, but after a while Marlon Peters grumbled from behind a book: 'Miss, that man too racial, miss.'

'What was that, Peters?' asked Miss Hafeez.

Goody-goody Alicia Henderson, who was always ready to carry news, and who sat right up under the teacher's table, reported: 'Miss, he say Mr Tewarie too racial, miss.'

Children nodded and murmured in agreement.

'And what is the meaning of this word "racial," class? That doesn't say very much. If you want to accuse Mr Tewarie of something, then the least you can do is get the right word. What is it you're saying about your Spanish teacher?'

There was a brief hush, then some snickers. Then

Doreen Sandiford shot up brazenly and said in her loud, hoarse voice: 'Miss, he don't like black-hen chicken, miss. He does only show us bad-face, like if them Indian children doesn't play tricks in class, too, miss.'

Everybody was giggling from the time she said 'black-hen chicken,' but now Miss held up her hand for us to stop. Just at that moment, however, Marlon Peters was saying, behind his book, to his fans around him: 'My father say the only good coolie is a dead coolie,' and everybody heard, so everybody started laughing again.

Miss was shaking her head weakly from side to side. The gang of boys at the back now seemed to be having their own private joke. Miss held up both her hands for all the noise to stop, and right away Marlon Peters stood up to speak, with Anand Persad trying to pull him back down into the chair: 'Miss, Persad say . . .'

Persad tried to clamp his hand over Peters's mouth. Peters grabbed both of Persad's arms and held him in a tight, struggling hug while he rattled off, as fast as he could: 'Miss, Persad say he uncle tell him he want to go in South Africa and help them white people kill-out nigger.'

Miss Hafeez was a small lady, but very tough, usually. Yet now, while Peters and Persad boxed each other playfully and we laughed with glee, we saw her sink into her chair, holding her heart and gasping: 'Lord have mercy!'

The laughing died down, because Miss looked really stricken. We stared at her and she at us. We hoped that Mr Tewarie was forgotten.

'Well,' she breathed. 'I don't know what to say. But I will tell you that the word for all of that is not "racial." It is "racist." And it is not a laughing matter.'

'"Racist", miss?' someone asked. 'Miss, "racist" is like over in America, or South Africa, miss. Like them Klu Klee ... Klu Klu ... Klu Klux Klan and thing. We not so, miss.'

The class agreed. 'Racist' was the word for those wicked white people in South Africa and America. In our country we just had some people who were *racial*.

Miss held her head and looked frantic: 'What you mean "just"? People talking about killing off one another and you laugh *kya-kya* and you say "just"! That is not "just" anything, that is *racism*, children, and it is dangerous! You really think it can be all right to want one another dead?'

Miss obviously found this offence much, much worse than whatever we had done to Mr Tewarie.

'Look,' she said. 'All the *dooglas* in the class, stand up – everybody with one parent of Indian descent and the other of African descent.'

About five children stood up. Marlon Peters bobbed up and down, and one of his gang reported: 'Miss, Peters say he's a half-doogla, miss. He grandfather was a Indian.'

'Okay, Peters, stand up if that is true. Any more "half-*dooglas*"?'

Two girls stood up.

'Now,' said Miss. 'I saw all of you laughing and skinning your teeth just now. So you think it would be a big joke if one side of your family were to kill off the other side, eh?'

'No, miss,' they droned, for there didn't seem to be much else to be said.

'Or, we could just divide the whole class into "coolie" and "nigger" and let one half kill off the other –' Miss stopped abruptly. 'But the two of you still think it's a joke!'

We looked around, and Peters and Persad were shooting imaginary guns at each other. We didn't laugh too loudly, for we knew that Miss would get even more upset.

Everybody was relieved that she had gone off the topic of Mr Tewarie, and now, luckily, the bell rang before she could get back to it.

She still hadn't seen about roll call.

'Who is absent, apart from Anjanee?' she asked, hurriedly filling out the register.

As she got up to go, she made as if to say something to us; but then she only shook her head sadly, and left.

I went home on weekends until about the middle of the term. Then my father put his foot down.

One Friday morning, with my bag already packed, I went to Miss Velma for the bus fare as usual.

'I forget to tell you, darling. Your father say he not sending you home this weekend. He give somebody the message for your grandmother already.'

Not sending me home? Mr Cephas was keeping me here in this house for the weekend? I rested my bag of clothes on a chair, and opened my mouth to protest. But what was the use of protesting to Miss Velma? It was Mr Cephas who was preventing me from going home. He had left poor Miss Velma to give me the news and he was safely out of the house. Miss Velma looked so sorrowful that I could not say anything to make her feel worse.

'All right, Miss Velma,' I said, and took the clothes back into the bedroom.

I went to school. Sitting in class, I could think of nothing but how to get away for the weekend.

I worked out scheme after scheme. I would go on the bus and tell the driver that he would get his money next week ... I would go home at lunchtime and beg Miss Velma to lend me the bus fare ... I would go to Ma Zelline ... Aha! Ma Zelline! She would surely help me ... and my grandmother would surely break my bones for harassing Ma Zelline and, worst of all, asking for money!

Ma had told me to go and find Ma Zelline if I was in trouble. 'But only if you in *real* trouble,' she had added. What she meant by *real* trouble she never said, but I knew it was to do with my father. Ma thought my father might do something really terrible to me, something she couldn't even talk about. I only saw it in her face every now and then as she questioned me about how he was treating me.

'I not sending you to harass the lady with every little stupidness, but you know that she will help you if something happen. Zelline don't want no child round her neck.'

If Ma Zelline wanted children she would have made some, Ma said. Or, her sister had about twenty hungry children and she could have taken any one of them that she wanted. 'But who say just because you name Woman you must mind child? Not Zelline!'

Ma and my mother often talked about Ma Zelline. I heard Ma say that there were ignorant people in this world who counted a woman as nothing if she didn't have children. But Zelline, she said, was the rightest one for them.

One of the stories I'd heard them tell was about how once, in the heat of a quarrel, another woman had taunted Ma Zelline about not having children: she called Ma Zelline a 'mule'. Ma Zelline gathered up her skirt, pushed her face in the other woman's face, and said: 'Yes. Look the mule!' and turning around swiftly, she fired a terrible kick, backwards, at the woman.

I had not been to see Ma Zelline since the day we came to town to register. It would be so good to visit her, not to ask for anything, but just to listen to her talk, look at her books, stroll through her flower garden. She would be glad to see me, I knew. If I couldn't go home for the weekend, maybe I would pay Ma Zelline a visit ...

Anjanee slid into her seat next to me, flustered and puffing. I would wait till break time to tell her how Mr Cephas planned to tie my foot for the weekend.

'So what you going to do?' Anjanee asked, her eyes wide with concern.

'Nothing,' I said. I was calmer now. Spending the weekend in town wouldn't be so bad if I could visit Ma Zelline. Mr Cephas was never home, and I could get Miss Velma to send me to the market or something. I would stay and make the best of a bad situation.

And my 'bad situation' was nothing compared to Anjanee's! Here she was, ready to take on my troubles when she had so much to worry about – too much for one person.

One of Anjanee's worries right now was the midterm test coming up the following week. She had missed so many days that what we were doing in class now was like gibberish to her, and she didn't have all the textbooks to study and catch up. I had lent her my geography book to take home overnight.

'You learn the geography?'

'I read a part in the bus going home yesterday. But

this morning I couldn't get to read again – the bus was full and I had to stand up.

'Okay. Lunchtime we will learn it,' I promised. 'And then you will carry home the science book for the weekend.'

We wandered along the corridors until the bell rang.

That same Friday evening Mr Cephas came home so early that he startled Miss Velma.

I was sitting at the dining-room table doing my homework, mainly revising for the midterm test. My mind was not on the work. I kept thinking of home and what everybody would be doing. The little children would be very disappointed when I didn't turn up.

Ma might be worried. Mr Cephas had sent a message, yes, but Ma didn't trust my father. She might be so worried that she might send Uncle Leroy for me.

When I heard the car outside, my spirits lifted for a moment. I thought, wishfully, that it might be Uncle Leroy and Jai.

Rampie's son Jai, who was a mechanic, had an old, sprawling, rusty American car that Pappy called a 'moving accident'. Jai liked to tell people how a Yankee fella working down at the oil company had paid him five dollars to just drive the old junk away, out of his sight forever.

The whole of the Balatier football team would pack into Jai's car when they had to go and play a match against another village. Every now and then

Uncle Leroy and Jai, and some other men and women from Sooklal Trace, would get into the car and go liming in Junction, or La Puerta. Sometimes they would even put God out of their thoughts and drive all the way to the city in Jai's sputtering old junk ...

But it was not Uncle Leroy, only Mr Cephas, coming through the door with a nervous smile on his face. I said 'Good evening' and turned to my books again.

'Doing your home lesson, eh?'

'Yes,' I said, with a face that put an end to all conversation.

Michael crept in through the back door. He had come home from school and disappeared again shortly afterwards to God knows where. Sometimes he went to a neighbour's house to watch television. Wherever he was, he must have seen Mr Cephas's car and sped home.

'Good evening, Daddy,' he panted.

'So where you now coming from, mister?'

'Nowhere, Daddy.'

'Get your book and do your home lesson!'

Michael dived into the bedroom and came out again with his schoolbag.

For the next hour or so, he sat at the table with a copybook in front of him, fidgeting, scratching his legs, and turning pages, until Miss Velma came to set the table and put him out of his misery.

Mr Cephas did not change his clothes and go back out again. Instead, he stayed home and cleaned his car. When he had eaten, he still did not go out. He sat in the drawing room, studying a newspaper.

Miss Velma and I cleared the table. I knew that

my father had come home early to make sure that I was there, and was staying home to prevent me from escaping. Once or twice he cleared his throat and shot me a glance as if he wanted to start a conversation with me but didn't know how.

The next morning I got up and washed my clothes. Then I helped Miss Velma with the housework. Mr Cephas woke up at about ten o'clock and peeped out at me as I was sweeping the drawing room. I said 'Good morning', as politely as I could.

Mr Cephas sat down to eat and then started shouting at Michael to get out of bed and take up his book. Michael appeared, dazed, at the bedroom door.

'Boy!' Mr Cephas snapped. 'What is your ambition!'

'I don't know, Daddy,' Michael replied.

'You don't know? You damn right you don't know! And I don't know why I feeding you and clothing you and spending money on you. Money that I work hard for. Why I should feed you and clothe you, boy? What you doing to earn your keep?'

'Nothing, Daddy.'

'Yes! Nothing self! Well, from this weekend you going to start to earn your keep. I not feeding any loafers and ingrates and all who think I does pick money off a tree. Go and wash your face and take up your book!'

Mr Cephas ate his fill and got up. After a long spell in the bathroom and an even longer time moving about in the bedroom, he was stepping out through the front door, smartly dressed and smelling sweet, and still patting his hair down. It was clear that he was really going *out*, and not just around the corner. This was my time to go and visit Ma Zelline.

'So, *ti-mamzelle*. All this time you staying in La Puerta and not one day you can't say let me go and see if the old *soucouyant* dead or alive?'

Ma Zelline was trying to look stern, but her eyes, as always, were full of laughter.

'My grandmother say not to bother you . . .'

'And what *you* say? You find is botheration if you come and see me now and then?'

'No, Ma Zelline.'

'All right. So tell me what you doing in school. You studying your books? What they teaching you up there?'

Soon I was telling Ma Zelline all about our battles with the Circus-horse, the antics of Marlon Peters and his gang, Mr Tewarie, Anjanee . . .

She was interested in everything. She filled her pipe and settled back to listen, mostly chuckling at the stories that I told.

But when I told her about Anjanee, a cloud came over her face. She stopped puffing at her pipe and stared at me grimly. Then her eyes seemed to be looking straight past me as she shook her head from side to side.

'*Bonjay*, Lord God!' she said to herself. 'That

poor little girl will do something one day; and then all of them will hold they head and bawl.'

We sat in a heavy silence until Ma Zelline put her pipe in her mouth again and sucked on it.

'So what about Cephas, now,' she inquired, adding under her breath: 'That old nastiness.'

I told her that my father was well.

'Yes, I know he well, he always well – God ain't ready for he yet. I want to know if you well. He treating you properly, or he take you to make servant?'

I didn't know where to start, but the next thing I knew, vexation was tumbling out of me. I was talking very fast and almost at the top of my voice. 'I will stay there to go to school, but I don't want to stay there for the weekend! I want to go home, or else I not staying there!'

Ma Zelline gently laid a hand on my arm.

'Come,' she said. 'Let's go and get some juice, and then you will tell me about this thing.'

I followed her into the kitchen, where she poured two large enamel mugs of guava juice and listened to my tale of woe.

'*Salaud!* The stingy dog!' Ma Zelline fumed. 'Just the two-cents for you to pay the bus to go home. Don't want to put he hand in he pocket. *Salaud*. Not to worry with that, you hear, child? You just study your book, and one day you will have your own money. You will never have to ask no man for nothing. Well, I do declare! When he keep you here for the weekend, you just come and look for me, you hear, and take your mind off of he.'

I wasn't so sure what my father would think of

that arrangement, but I promised Ma Zelline that I would come and see her. Then I thought I would take my leave, but Ma Zelline had other plans.

'So what we eating for lunch? I wasn't cooking today – pot turn down. Is so when you living in bachie, you could turn down your pot when you want. Nobody to say "Zelline, where my food? Zelline, I hungry . . ." But today I have *guest*!'

It was funny to hear Ma Zelline talk about herself as 'living in bachie'. I had somehow thought that only a man's place could be called a bachie. That was what Uncle Leroy called his room, which had its own door and steps to the outside, and where we were not allowed unless he invited us in. He had built this room, with the help of his friends, on to the side of our house.

'I better go back now. I don't know when Mr Cephas coming home, and he might be vex,' I explained.

'*Vex*? You gone by your grandmother *ma com-mère* – you gone by Zelline. Ma Zelline is your grandmother good, good friend. So you gone by your family – Cephas can't be so drunk as to vex with you for that. Come we jook down a breadfruit and make some oildown. Vex? Cephas know *how* you grow and get big? He know where you get food to eat till now? I don't know why your grandmother take you and give you to that worthless man. He don't deserve to have no child like you, to tell people about "my daughter, my daughter." Since when he know he have daughter? Look here! . . .' Ma Zelline now fretted to herself in patois as she marched me off towards the back door.

We went out through the door and round to the side of the house where there was a big breadfruit tree. Ma Zelline sighted a breadfruit that was about the size of my head, and just the right shade of green for picking. Using Ma Zelline's long bamboo rod with the cocoa knife at the top, we jabbed at its stem until the breadfruit came crashing down through the leaves of the tree. It fell with a loud thud, but it was firm enough and did not burst. In an old tub under the eave of the house Ma Zelline had a forest of herbs growing, and she picked some leaves of thyme while I went in search of a green pepper. Then we went into the front yard to cut some dasheen bush to put on top of everything in the pot – breadfruit, salt meat, seasoning, and coconut milk. Ma Zelline cut some leaves, then dug up a dasheen as well, which she weighed in her hand with pride.

She moved around slowly and contentedly, and we chatted as we went. She wanted to know how my grandmother was, and then everybody else in the family.

'How your mammy, you writing to her?'

I told her how my mother had started to go to high school in New York.

'Well, praise God! I did always tell Patsy, "Don't mind you miss your chance as a young girl, you have your brains. You will get a chance again, and when you get it, is to take it." Praise God!'

Ma Zelline straightened up from bending over the dasheen patch. 'And you, now. You have the best chance. You see and do good! Don't mind no Cephas, no Circus-horse ... That dotish Velma and all will put a blight on you. Look how hard your mammy have to work to get a little education, and you get it right in your hand. Don't throw away that!'

The midterm test began on Monday morning. Spanish was first. Anjanee arrived so late that I had already finished translating the ten silly sentences about Mummy in the supermarket, Daddy in his office, and Sister at the hairdresser's. I was reading a book.

Mr Tewarie was reading, too. I could see from his face that it was one exciting newspaper. His mouth was hanging open, and he wasn't looking at us at all. So as soon as Anjanee sat down I placed my translation where she could see it.

At break time Anjanee was sick with fright: maths was next. We were walking back to the classroom when the bell rang, and Anjanee suddenly turned and started to run in the opposite direction. I caught up with her outside; she was bent over a drain, vomiting.

We got back to the classroom about five minutes late. The Circus-horse was giving out question papers, and she stopped with a paper in mid-air: 'So where Miss Mastana Bahar and her shadow just coming from, may I ask?'

A few children giggled and then fell silent.

'Anjanee was feeling sick,' I informed Mrs Lopez curtly as I helped Anjanee get into her seat.

She continued to glare at us for a moment, then sucked her teeth and went on giving out papers. Anjanee's face was grey. As she read through the question paper, she trembled and twisted her fingers together.

I knew that this was one test I could not help her with, for Mrs Lopez would be watching us like a hawk.

Before the end of the week we began to get our test results. The Circus-horse walked heavily and re-proachfully into the classroom one day. She dropped our pile of test papers on to the table and stared at us as if she were too offended to even talk.

We knew that we would have to suffer a speech before we could hear our marks. So we settled back and waited for the worst.

'I don't know what some of you doing here. I don't know. You think that secondary school is just wash-your-foot-and-jump-in? No! Secondary school is for people with *brains*. Some of you have no business here.'

She glared at Marlon Peters, Anjanee, and a few others around the class. Marlon Peters smiled broadly and turned his head from side to side, bowing, as though he were surrounded by cheering crowds.

'You see?' Mrs Lopez exploded. 'Look at that grinning fool! He should go and sing calypso, not come here for people to hurt their head trying to teach him something that will uplift him. And take Miss Jugmohansingh now – always sleeping in class, when she is here at all. Girl, why you don't just stay home and help them make garden?' (Mrs Lopez pronounced it *gyaarden*, to make fun of the way people like us spoke.) 'You have no use for secondary school. Five percent – five marks out of a hundred – that is what Miss Jugmohansingh made in my maths test. And the calypsonian? Four. Four out of a hundred ...'

Anjanee sat with her head bowed, still as a statue, while Mrs Lopez read out everybody's marks, except mine.

What had I done to this lady now? What special torture did she have in store for me?

She paused and started to arrange her face into a pleasant expression. When she had succeeded, she turned this pleasant expression on *me!*

'Laetitia Johnson: 98 percent,' she announced, and she held up my paper as the class went into a chorus of *oos* and *ahs*, and even some whistles. Mrs Lopez realized that this would get out of hand in a second, and brought it to a swift end by changing back into her normal, scornful face.

'See me afterwards, Laetitia Johnson,' she ordered when there was silence. 'Now we will go over the test paper.'

Later Mrs Lopez talked to me in the conference room which students called the 'Courthouse'. (Some called it the 'Latrine', for it was said that students could get a sudden running-belly when they were summoned there by teachers.)

'You are a bright girl,' Mrs Lopez said in a coaxing voice. 'You are way above those other children. So you have to be careful if you want to get ahead, you hear? Pick your friends – don't mix up with any and everybody. They will want to drag you down with them. You make sure and stay far from these children – they have no ambition . . .'

The Circus-horse talked on and on, and the more she talked, the more determined I became: I would show this woman that I was no friend of hers.

I had not seen Mr Cephas since the weekend, for he came in quite late the first few nights of that week. I was usually in the bedroom by then, reading or getting ready for bed. The table was always set and waiting for him, and at whatever hour he arrived, Miss Velma would shuffle out to the kitchen to warm his food.

One evening he had came home while I was still at the dining-room table, studying for the geography test. I heard the car come in, and he was on his way up the steps when he seemed to slow down. Then he was calling to Miss Velma from the gallery, in a stern voice, to bring the newspapers for him. He didn't come in to eat until much later, when I was already dropping off to sleep.

On Thursday night I packed my bag for the weekend. Everybody would be so proud of my midterm test results. Pappy might make a speech. Ma would only say 'Hmph,' but a little smile would be pulling at the corner of her mouth. Uncle Leroy might do *anything* – give me a sip of beer, let me ride his bicycle out the Trace and back, or make some funny toy for me out of wood and wire and crown corks (or maybe he would think I was getting too big for that now).

The test was over and there was no homework. It was still early, so I would be able to lie in bed and read for a while.

Then Mr Cephas came home. He was much too early – I knew that this was a bad sign.

I heard him sit down in the drawing room and then get up again. He walked into the kitchen and then back out into the drawing room. After a few moments Miss Velma appeared over me. She whispered nervously that my father wanted to see me.

I came out with the book in my hand.

'Good evening,' I said.

'"Good evening," who? Your grandmother teach you to disrespect me, eh? "Good evening," dog, cat, who?' He was using the voice he used for Taking Michael in Hand.

"Good evening ... sir," I said. His mouth fell open – he almost gasped.

'"Sir"? Children calling their father "sir" now? You know that I am your father?'

'Yes ... Father,' I said, which didn't make him much happier. He seemed to give up.

'What you doing in the bedroom?'

'Reading ... Father.'

'You reading your schoolbook? You studying? Let me see – what is this, storybook?'

I nodded.

'Aha!' he said. 'You lying down in your bed reading storybook and Miss Velma in the kitchen with all the work! You going to be a worthless woman? That is how your mother and your grandmother bring you up?' He seemed to expect an answer, but I had none, and I simply stood and stared back at him. He shifted himself in the armchair. Then he cleared his throat.

'Look here,' he said. 'My house is not a hotel. You can't come here and lime for the week, and then weekend you pick up yourself and you gone. I don't have money for you to be joy-riding up and down the country. I doing my duty to feed you and clothe you and see about your schooling, not to send you joy-riding up and down the country. And for me to feed you and clothe you, you will have to stay and give a hand in this house.'

He fidgeted in his chair again, then bent down and began tying his shoelaces, or untying them, I wasn't sure which. He looked up and I was still standing rooted to the spot.

He tried to smile. 'You finish reading? Go ahead and done, na?'

So I stayed in Mr Cephas's house for the weekend again. And again nobody came to rescue me and take me home – no Uncle Leroy, no Ma. I didn't go to see Ma Zelline, because that would be harassing her, to find myself in her house one weekend after another. In any case, this weekend, Mr Cephas did not go out much, or for very long. He stayed at home for hours on end, shouting at Michael and now and then trying to start a conversation with me.

He complained to me that Michael was a wayward boy and not learning anything at school, and how he wished that Michael could be more like his big sister. He praised me for the neatness of the drawing room, which I had cleaned on Saturday morning. He asked me when were those teachers going to give us a test so I could get a chance to lick all the other children in the class, and I said I didn't know.

The following week I made sure to get every maths assignment wrong. I wrote neatly, drew tidy margins, and followed the method obediently up to a point when I thought it was time to spoil things. The Circus-horse was driven to despair.

Anjanee was in a worse state than ever. She had

failed almost everything in the midterm test. She had headaches all day long, and as usual she was tired from all the work she had to do at home. And the sadder she looked, the more Mrs Lopez trampled on her.

She started to talk about dropping out of school. I didn't know what to say to her. At first I took it lightly. 'Well, Lopez will be glad. She will give one big going-away party for you.'

Anjanee smiled a sad, tired smile. As the days passed I realized that she was really giving up. 'I only wasting taxi fare to come here. Better I stay home and help my mother. I not learning nothing.'

'You mad or what! You can't leave school now! After you fight-up to pass Common Entrance and you reach in here, you going to throw away your chance just so?'

'I don't have no chance again, Lacey. I too far behind. For me to catch up I would have to take lessons, and where I getting money for that?'

Lessons! That was it! After-school lessons every day. Anjanee's bus didn't leave until four o'clock. We could study together every day after school.

'I will give you lessons, Anjanee. We will stay back every day and do some work together.'

She opened her eyes wide. 'What your father will say when you reaching home late every day? That will only make trouble for you.'

'*Steups*. He reaching home six, seven, eight o'clock and all. And Miss Velma, I will just tell her I staying back to study with a friend. She not going to make no trouble.'

So we sat in the classroom on afternoons and

worked together until it was time for Anjanee to catch her bus. In every subject Anjanee seemed to be starting from scratch, and she was so tired and sleepy that she could hardly think.

After our sessions I walked to the bus station with her and then sped home. One never knew with Mr Cephas – any day he might suddenly decide to come home straight from work.

I was getting home well after four o'clock on afternoons, and Miss Velma was not too comfortable with this arrangement. She pleaded with me to be careful.

Bit by bit Anjanee's work started to improve. One day in geography class the teacher handed back our exercise books, and when Anjanee opened hers, her whole face lit up. She passed the book over to me with a broad, grateful smile: she had got six marks out of ten!

It was clear now that Mr Cephas was never going to give me bus fare to go home again. Another weekend passed and I remained, stranded, in La Puerta. I wrote a letter to Ma asking what I should do.

I hoped, of course, that she would send somebody right away to pick me up, and to tell off my father for trying to keep me away from home. But days passed and nothing of the sort happened.

Then a letter came from Uncle Leroy. Ma's instructions were to stay where I was until the Christmas holidays, which were now only a few weeks away. She had enclosed bus fare, but only for an emergency.

Right away I got into trouble at school. The Circus-horse gave us an assignment to do in class, and at the end of the period I handed up a perfectly blank page, with my name and address – Sooklal Trace, Balatier – written neatly in the top right-hand corner.

In the next period I joined with Marlon Peters and Naushad Ali in one of their plots to drive Mr Tewarie out of his mind.

Miss Hafeez summoned us to the conference room.

'Laetitia,' she said drily. 'These two gentlemen *love* this room, so they always doing something to get inside here. Peters and Ali *living* in here. But you – what you doing here?'

With Miss Hafeez one did not give a rude and foolish answer like 'You say to meet you here, miss.' There was nothing about her that made you feel like stepping out of line. Miss Hafeez did not tolerate any nonsense, and we knew that it was because she was on our side. She wanted us to do well.

If the two foolish boys had not been there, I would have explained everything to Miss Hafeez. But it was no business of these two fools that I wanted to go home and was not allowed to. That would just be one more Joke for their clown show.

So I just laid my complaints against the Circus-horse and Mr Tewarie.

'Miss, when she come in the class she does look at us as if she smelling something bad. And she too unfair. She does treat Anjanee like if she is some dog, and Anjanee never trouble the lady at all. And she don't bother to explain nothing when the children don't understand the maths. She ain't care about us. As for Mr Tewarie – we don't learn a thing in his class. He is a living dead.'

Marlon and Naushad were nodding furiously while I spoke. They wanted to add their piece, but Miss Hafeez stopped them.

'All right. Listen to me. Make this the last time I get any bad reports about any of you from these teachers. You don't have to like all your teachers, but you have to do your work and get out of here. When you play the fool you don't harm the teachers, you harm yourself. Don't give them cause to report you again, because then we'll have to discuss the matter with your parents. That means you, too, Miss Johnson. You *really* messing yourself up, girl, and if you don't stop, your parents will have to know.'

One afternoon when I got home my father was there already, waiting for me. I didn't know it, but he had just seen me outside the bus station where Anjanee and I always lingered for a few minutes before she got on the bus.

Of course, he wanted to know what business I had over there, and my explanation did not please him one bit. I could not care less.

'So you playing woman now. You could just go where you want, when you want? And out of all the children it have in that big school, the only thing you could find to friend with is a *coolie*?'

He ranted and raved, and I stared at him coldly. Miss Velma was hiding somewhere, terrified.

'... This is a decent house, and so long as you living here you will behave like decent people. And decent girls don't go knocking all about the town. You want to play hot-foot? Not here. Not here at all. When you see school over, you just find yourself home one time! I going to check up on you. You hear me!'

'Yes, Mr Cephas.'

He nearly choked. 'Right! Good! Give me your damn rudeness! Who is "Mr Cephas"? Eh? Who you calling "Mr Cephas"! God does punish ungratefulness, you hear!'

We stared at each other for a moment, and then he seemed to sag in his chair, like a bundle of old clothes.

'Go and help your stepmother,' he said, wearily.

That was the end of after-school lessons. I convinced Anjanee that we could cut some of Mr Tewarie's classes to continue working together. Mr Tewarie wouldn't even miss us. Many children were absent every Spanish class and he didn't seem to notice, or care.

We sat on a little bench behind the music room. Anjanee didn't like the idea of cutting classes, and she was very jumpy. She tried her best to concentrate, but now nothing stuck in her head, and she was falling further and further behind every day.

Once I lost my patience with her over a simple maths operation that she could not remember, no matter how many times I showed her the steps. In the end I heard myself shouting at her: 'But everybody learn this for Common Entrance, man! And you sit Common Entrance *twice*! How you don't know it yet! Try, na man, try!'

Anjanee's eyes filled up with tears. 'You see!' she said. 'I tell you I can't learn.'

'I didn't mean it so, Anjanee, I didn't mean it so. Come, let's start over.'

But the day was already spoiled.

*

I was still at war with the Circus-horse, although I had to be careful not to do anything that she could report me for. The new plan that I hit upon was to do all her assignments right for two days and get a hundred on everything, followed by two days of zero; then I would go back up to a hundred, then back down to zero, and so on. The Circus-horse washed her hands of me.

If only Mr Cephas would also wash his hands of me! I couldn't understand why he didn't just send me home. I had nothing to say to him but 'Good morning' and 'Good night', and he was full of vexation all the time now.

He couldn't find anything to scold me for. Whenever he was at home, I was either in the kitchen with Miss Velma or at the dining-room table poring over my schoolbooks. I only read in bed when he was out.

He couldn't find any reason to quarrel with me, but he growled at Miss Velma all the time; he made Michael read nearly every night and hit him with the book when he stalled. He made long, angry speeches about how much food was wasted in his house, and how many lights were left on carelessly without any regard for who was paying the light bill, and how some people thought that money grew on trees. Why, for the life of me, didn't he just send me home!

I had made up my mind that I wasn't coming back to this house. When I went home for the Christmas vacation I would persuade Ma not to send me back. I would go to school from Sooklal Trace even if it meant getting up in what Ma called 'foreday morning' and *walking* all the way to Junction to meet the bus.

Meanwhile, I would have to work on getting a good report to take home to Ma's house. She had not put a licking on me since I was ten years old, but there was no reason to believe that she wouldn't do it now.

I began to go regularly to Spanish class. Mr Tewarie was still a dead loss and I could learn all the Spanish I needed from the book. But I didn't want him writing in my report book that I had been cutting classes. I was even polite to the Circus-horse, and I started doing her assignments properly again.

The end-of-term exam was near, and Anjanee and I studied together at lunchtime, at break time, and even for a little time after school. Mr Cephas could check up on me all he wanted to. Soon I would be out of his reach forever.

I was fully packed and ready to go two weeks before the end of term. I had it all planned. I would take one bag to school with me on the last day of term. I would use the bus fare Ma had sent to go home. Then during the vacation Uncle Leroy would come to La Puerta and fetch the rest of my belongings.

The Christmas breeze was softening my father's mood. Parang music was in the air, and carols, and all the jingles about Christmas shopping. Miss Velma was sewing cushions and curtains; the nextdoor neighbours were painting, and the people opposite had colourful flashing lights strung into the branches of the Julie mango tree in their front yard.

Mr Cephas brought home a steady stream of cronies for a 'Christmas drink', and he was in high spirits all the time.

'So you spending Christmas with your daddy and your Tantie Velma for the first time, eh?' he said to me one evening, stopping short of putting his arm around me.

'No,' I answered. 'I going home.'

His face fell, and he said in a dull voice: 'All right. I will drop you down Saturday.'

'No, is okay. I taking the bus.'

'What!' he snapped. 'For your grandmother to wash her mouth on me? Just get yourself ready and wait for me Saturday after lunch. That old b— that lady will not have it to say that Orville Cephas is a this and Orville Cephas is a that. Not at all.'

I did not fancy the long drive to Sooklal Trace alone in the car with him again, so I asked if Michael could come, too. Mr Cephas agreed and Michael was overjoyed – as soon as his father went out of the room he threw his dusty arms around me and hugged me tight. He smelled like a ram-goat, but I couldn't spoil his happiness by telling him to go and bathe.

The end-of-term exam came. Anjanee did a little better in some of the subjects, but she knew that she was still failing.

We were having a class party on the last day of term. Everyone was asked to bring something to eat or drink. Anjanee, very flustered, said she would bring something to drink. Afterwards she went to Miss Hafeez and told her that she was not coming to the party because she had no money to buy anything.

Miss Hafeez asked her whether she had any sour lemons in her yard.

'Well, you bring some sour lemons, and we will go in the home-ec room and make lemonade for everybody.'

We decorated the classroom with balloons and paper streamers and flowers. Miss Hafeez told us she was keeping our report books until after the party, for she wanted everybody to have a good time.

We did. Even Anjanee looked bright and cheerful.

Marlon Peters and his gang put on a little play about school. We laughed so much we were almost rolling on the floor.

Marlon Peters had smuggled his big sister's clothes out of the house – all her clothes, it seemed. He wore about three skirts of different colours, one on top of the other, and any number of blouses. His wrists were crowded with bangles – real ones and ones he had made out of wire, plastic, twine, anything. Around his neck, too, he wore a bunch of 'necklaces' of every description.

His face was heavily powdered with flour, and he had smeared bright red lipstick on his mouth and cheeks. There was so much stuff painted around his eyes that they looked like a panda's eyes. Somebody in his family had played in the Carnival band 'Warriors of the Amazon' and he was wearing the headpiece: a wig made of hanging black string. Two colourful Christmas-tree decorations were tied on to the headpiece, on either side of his face, for earrings.

He also wore stockings (which were slowly sliding down his legs) and carried a handbag.

Marlon Peters wobbled in on tall-heeled, pointed shoes, with his nose in the air, carrying some exercise books. He flung the exercise books down on the floor and gave a long speech in a ridiculous lady-voice:

'Take allyu old nasty books and get away from me! Allyu have no right in here – your head too hard, you too dunce, you too ugly, you too black, you have no manners, you have no parents. I don't even want to *see* allyu. I am going for the principal!'

And he wobbled out to wild applause, just as one of his grandmother's stockings finally flopped down around his ankle.

After the party Miss Hafeez distributed report books. Anjanee was afraid to open hers, so I didn't look into mine, either.

I walked with Anjanee to the bus station.

'That was a nice party,' she said, grinning as broadly as she had done on the first day of school.

'Yes, girl,' I answered, and I did a few mincing steps with my head in the air like the Circus-horse. We held our sides and shrieked with laughter, remembering Marlon Peters's outfit.

'And you ain't see the stockings!' Anjanee gasped, sending us into more peals of laughter. We had to wipe our eyes with a handkerchief.

'That old *soucouyant*,' I said, when I was able to talk again. 'Next term we will show her maths! Next term you getting ninety-nine point nine percent in that lady maths test, wait you see.

'Lacey, how I getting ninety-nine point nine percent in Mrs Lopez maths, you know how to do magic, eh? We going and work *obeah* on she?' We folded up with laughter again.

'No, child. You forget I not coming back by Cephas. From next term we could study every day after school, because I taking bus, too!'

'Oho,' she said, looking thoughtful. 'You lucky, yes.'

'I don't want to see he again, in my whole life. I don't know how my mother coulda ever friend with a foolish man like that.'

117

A mischievous look came over Anjanee's face. She put her hand over her mouth and leaned towards my ear: 'They was in love!'

'*Anjanee!*' She darted away as I swung my bag at her.

'Anyway,' she said, trying to make her face serious and wise, 'I mustn't talk big-people talk with little children. You ain't get your monthly yet.'

'So you get yours?'

'Yep,' she said.

I felt a blow of sadness, as though Anjanee had taken one big step away from me.

'You getting yours any day now,' she said in a comforting voice. We were quiet for a time.

'Suppose I had a different name,' she said suddenly.

I was puzzled. 'Like what?'

'Like Anjanee Maharaj, or Narinesingh, or something ...' She was looking at me and smiling her first-day-of-school smile, and I knew what she meant. I remembered how the principal had paired us off by calling our names in alphabetical order.

'Then you mighta get Marlon Peters for your partner instead, and the two of you woulda married!'

'*Lacey!*' she scolded, and I had to lean up on a wall so as not to collapse with laughing.

The station was still some distance away, and we had to stop skylarking now, or Anjanee might miss her bus. We sobered up and walked on, arm-in-arm, pondering on the months just past.

'So you make a whole term, eh, Anjanee?' She nodded gravely. I knew that she still had not opened her report book. 'You didn't do so bad in the exam. Next term we will show them!'

Anjanee's face had become solemn again, but she was still in good spirits. She got on the bus and I stood and waved.

'Next term!' I shouted. 'Next term!'

Through the window of the moving bus Anjanee shouted back at me: 'Happy Christmas!'

All the teachers had written words of glowing praise in my report book, even the Circus-horse. I would take it to show Ma Zelline – I was going to visit her in the morning, to wish her Happy Christmas before I left for home.

Late in the evening Mr Cephas asked to see my report book. It threw him into a state of excitement. He wanted to keep it to show his boss on Monday morning.

He couldn't, however, because it was addressed to 'Mrs Wilhemina Johnson, Sooklal Trace, Balatier.'

For the drive home I sat in the back seat with Michael, who chatted all the way, but under his breath. He glanced at his father nervously every now and then. Mr Cephas, however, was paying us no mind at all and never once turned his head around. He seemed bent on getting the task over and done with. When we reached our house, he off-loaded me and paid only the briefest of visits, much to Michael's disappointment.

Coming home again after such a long time, it was as though I was seeing our house for the first time. The board walls seemed to have mildewed a great deal while I was away. Uncle Leroy's addition, which he and his friends had built when I was in Standard Two, looked unfinished. The grey mortar seemed to be spilling out between the red-clay bricks.

Our bathroom and latrine seemed to have moved farther away from the house. Everything – the house, the kitchen, the bathroom, the latrine, the pigpen – looked a little rickety and old.

Ruth and Kenwyn were taller. Ruth was helping to carry water now, in a paint tin. Before I went to La Puerta I was carrying two buckets of water at a time – one on my head and one in my hand. Now just one bucket seemed a very heavy thing, and I had to stop and rest for a while.

Carlyle was very glad to see me, for while I was away he had had to carry extra buckets of water, sweep the yard, and collect wood for the fireside, all on top of his own work. Uncle Leroy had even made him weed my garden.

For days I got up early and walked down into the land, inspecting everything.

On the first morning, down in the garden with Uncle Leroy, I announced that I was not going back to my father's house.

'Oho, so you leaving school now?' he asked, without stopping what he was doing.

'No, I going to school from here.'

Uncle Leroy was still not very impressed. 'You tell your grandmother yet?'

'No, Uncle.'

'Hm,' he said. 'You want to come back here and eat green-fig? You living in a nice house, you driving in motorcar, eating food that they buy in the grocery – and you want to live here instead of there? You ain't have sense, girl!'

'I don't care, I want to come home,' I said sulkily.

'And how you reaching to school? Where you getting taxi fare and bus fare, you working somewhere?'

'No, Uncle, but I could get a bus pass.'

'Yes, and how you getting from here to Junction to get the bus? You will show the taxi man the bus pass, and he will carry you free!'

'No, Uncle, I not taking no taxi. I will take the bus to Junction.'

'You know what bus you talking about there? *One* bus it have passing here in the early morning, and you know what time it does pass? Quarter to six. What time you think you will have to get up to catch that bus?'

'I could get up early ...'

'Girl, behave yourself, you hear! Look at Carlyle. You don't think he would be glad to go and live in a pretty house in Puerta – no water to tote, no pigpen to clean ...'

I gave up. I would have to wait for the right moment to tackle Ma.

The Christmas work had begun – dusting, cobwebbing, scrubbing, polishing – and you could feel the excitement growing in our house.

Two days later Ma gathered together all her brass and went out into the gallery. She lined them up on the banister – vases, ashtrays, the big plant pot with a whole Bible story running around it, and a fruit bowl. Then she sat down to polish them with Brasso.

The smell of Brasso and floor polish and varnish meant Christmas. Ma was humming a Christmas hymn while she rubbed away. It seemed a good time to bring up the subject.

She did not seem surprised. Uncle Leroy must have spoken to her already.

'What it is happen with you and your father?' she asked, looking at me fixedly.

I couldn't point to anything that had 'happened.' It wasn't just that I missed coming home on weekends. I didn't want to stay in that house at all – not for one more day.

'What it is happen?' Ma insisted.

'Nothing, Ma' was all I could reply.

'Then why you can't stay there? What you running from?'

What could I say to them? I wanted to be home. I didn't want to live there.

When I didn't answer, Ma cut the discussion short with a few sharp words before turning back to her polishing: 'He is your father. He working for money. Let him mind you.'

One only argued with Ma inside one's head. I shouted, in my head, that I had been very well minded up until I left home, and that I didn't want anything more than I'd always had here at home. Mr Cephas's house, and his car and his money, meant nothing to me. I wanted to come home, dammit!

'I want to come home,' I heard myself saying meekly to Ma.

She stopped rubbing and looked at me for a few seconds. I couldn't tell what she was thinking. Then she dismissed me: 'Go and tell your grandfather,' she said, knowing full well that I would not dare to take what she called my 'stupidness' to Pappy. In any case, when Ma said no, even if Pappy were to say yes, the answer would still be no.

'And when you finish tell him, you could go and help Carlyle clean out under the house and burn the stuff. I never see so much old shoe, old paper, old cloth in my life. Under there getting like Balatier dumping-ground! Then allyu have the windows to wash, sorrel to pick, chairs to varnish ...' And she turned again to vigorously polishing her brass.

By the end of the week Ma had collected nearly all her army. Uncle Jamesie had brought up Jennifer, Junior, and Christine since the beginning of the holidays. Carlyle was sent to fetch his little brother. And on Friday, at nightfall, Ma's godson Anthony turned up, limping, hungry, and close to tears, with his clothes in a paper bag. His mother didn't have the money to pay his fare from Maitagual, which was about twenty miles away; so he had walked.

That weekend everybody helped to put away the house for Christmas. The whole place was dusted and scrubbed, mattresses and pillows hauled out into the sun, flower plants trimmed, and the yard mercilessly weeded and swept until it was bald. When we had finished sweeping the yard, the old cocoyea broom was in pieces. We had to strip some coconut branches and make a new one.

We varnished over the Morris chairs and the dining table, and on Christmas Eve we would polish the drawing-room floor. Uncle Leroy brought home a little tin of dark red paint, and a roll of linoleum, which he leaned up in a corner, to be put down in the gallery on Christmas Eve.

The paint was for the front steps. He had made us

scrub the steps the day before, until the concrete looked almost bleached, and nobody had been allowed to walk on them since then.

All the children stood around as he tackled the steps from the top. He wasn't sure that the paint would be enough for all five steps, so he was spreading it as thin as it could go.

We watched with pride and with excitement as our front steps, leading up into our gallery, slowly changed from pale grey concrete to a royal carpet of red.

We gathered closer as he moved down to the fourth step, and we held our breaths, for we saw then that there was only a little bit of paint left in the bottom of the pan. Uncle Leroy had stopped talking. We knew that we would also have to be quiet, and still, or he would snap at us, or chase us away.

The fourth step was finished. We now stood as still as statues, willing the paint to stretch to the last step. Uncle Leroy would pass the paintbrush all around the insides of the pan, and then wipe it on the step, again and again, until the brush was dry.

The top of the last step was covered. Now for the front and sides. He scraped around inside the pan, then wiped the concrete hard with the brush, stroke after stroke, until nothing more could come out of the brush.

In the end the paint tin was clean inside, and our front steps clothed in colour from top to bottom. Everybody shouted 'Ray!' and Uncle Leroy took off his cap and scratched his head.

'Well,' he said. 'When Lacey pass her high-school exam and get her big-work, she will buy paint and do the *whole house*. Not so, Lacey?' And all the children cheered loudly once again.

The front steps, of course, were now out of bounds until Christmas Eve.

The drawing room was bare, for the old curtains had been taken down, and the Morris chairs were lined up facing the wall for the varnish to dry. Their cushions, stripped of covers, were piled in a corner, waiting for Christmas Eve. Tantie Monica was sewing the new cushion covers, from the cloth Ma had bought since October, at a sale. The new curtains that Mammy Patsy had sent had not yet been brought forth.

There would be disorder for days, the worse the disorder the better, so that as darkness fell on Christmas Eve the house could turn, by magic, into a strange, rich place, bright with cleanness and newness.

In the days before Christmas, it was impossible to anger Ma. Children rolled on the mattresses put out to sun in the yard, or threw the pillows at each other. Asked to scrub down a chair, they would lose the soap in the bucket of water and end up more wet and soapy than the chair. Fights and loud squabbles broke out now and then, as in any other season. For all of this Ma only issued one threat, which we knew she could never bring herself to carry out: 'No Father Christmas!'

Our Christmas barrel from Mammy Patsy had already come. We knew that the big-people would have opened it and taken out the things to eat that might spoil. But after that they would have put the cover back and clamped it on with the iron ring, as though the barrel had never been opened. Now it was safely parked in a corner of Ma's bedroom, covered with a sheet.

There didn't seem to be enough Christmas work for Ma to do. When everything in sight had been dusted or scrubbed or polished until sore, she set upon our clothes – mending, sewing on buttons, letting down hems. This was not a good sign, for after the clothes, it was us: worm-oil for everyone, to clean out all the nastiness in our guts and make room for the Christmas eating.

It was Uncle Leroy who gave out worm-oil. Ma said she was too old now to fight children to get medicine down their throats. So, early one morning about a week before Christmas, Uncle Leroy roused us from our sleep and marched us out to the kitchen for worm-oil.

He was not moved by tears or pleas, and he could get the dose of evil-smelling, slimy oil through the most tightly clenched of teeth. Then we had to stay around the yard for the rest of the day and not eat anything. We were not to wander off into the land, where we might pick tangerines or guavas or whatever was bearing. By the end of the day we were so completely starved that we could only sit huddled on the back steps staring down at the kitchen.

That evening Uncle Leroy made an enormous coconut bake, with smoke herring, and melongene turned into beigan chokha, and we fell on it like the dogs.

It was time for Ma to make her Christmas journey to La Puerta. She was up and getting ready the next morning before we were properly out of bed. She wasn't going to buy anything in La Puerta, she announced in a loud voice, only a piece of cloth to put on the dining-room table so that Father Christmas wouldn't see how these children had scratched up her old mother's table till not even varnish could make it look pretty again. She was really going to La Puerta to pay Ma Zelline her Christmas visit, and on the way back she would stop off in Junction and pick up Charlene.

'But I not in no mood to argue with Maharajin. If she want to give me any speech, Leroy will have to go for his child for heself. First she want to give up the ghost because the daughter making Creole child – or 'kilwal' child, according to she – and she want to throw the two of them in the road. Now you nearly have to full-out application form to get to touch the 'kilwal' child. Eh-eh! That old lady must be have one thousand grandchildren. Is sixteen children Maharajin have! So she must be have grands till she forget they name! I can't understand why she must be so stingy with mine! Eh-eh!'

And Ma was off down the Trace. She wanted no tail behind her, not even as far as neighbour Phyllis's house. We were to stay and help Uncle Leroy, or 'No Father Christmas!'

Ma was gone for the whole day. Then at about four o'clock the news travelled up the Trace that she was on her way in. We hurriedly washed our feet and set out to meet her. Uncle Leroy went with us.

We heard Charlene's voice around a bend in the road before we saw them. She was chattering non-stop, and every now and then Ma would answer with a weary 'Mm-hmm,' or 'Yes, doo-doo.' Then we turned the bend and Charlene abandoned Ma to rush towards us, shrieking at the top of her voice: 'Uncle Leroy! Uncle Leroy! Everybody! Everybody! Look me! I come for Christmas!'

Uncle Leroy swept her up and hugged her and then seated her up on his shoulders. We took all of Ma's bags and bundles and made our way home with more commotion than Ma would usually allow.

When we got home Ma sat down heavily and sighed. After she had had her big enamel cup of water and we had taken turns fanning her, she began to tell Pappy about her visit to Ma Zelline.

'Look how Zelline want to spoil my Christmas,' she complained. 'I go there calling for my *macom-*

mère. No Zelline. Then a niece come out, and when I go inside, Zelline flat on her back with the sisters round her. That old-lady harden! The doctor tell her to keep herself quiet, but no, Zelline can't keep still. She gone out digging dasheen and get a bad-feel – fall down right there in the dasheen patch.'

Ma shook her head. 'That is a harden old-lady. She intend to dead standing up. She spending Christmas by one of her sisters, but she done start to tell them already that is only because is Christmas, and not because she sick, and if they think she leaving her house to go and live by any of them, they must be drunk. When Christmas done, she coming right back in her bachie.'

Ma chuckled and then looked worried again. 'Hm. Lacey girl, you mightn't find no Ma Zelline when you go back to Puerta!'

I didn't want to think of La Puerta at all, and worse yet, La Puerta with no Ma Zelline. But Ma was brightening up. All the children were hanging round to see what she had brought. She dug into one of her bags and fished out some balloons and whistles and then shooed us all away. The little ones ran out blowing whistles noisily, but Ma called Charlene back: 'Where you going in that dress, miss? Lacey, take that lady clothes for me, please.'

I took off Charlene's dress, her shoes, and her socks as quickly as I could, for she couldn't wait to run out into the yard with the others. When I had got everything off except her frilly panty, she rushed out joyfully, then rushed back in to hug Ma, burying her head in Ma's broad lap and trying to get her arms around her waist.

'Yes, my *doogla* baby,' Ma cooed. 'You tell your Nani you coming and live by your next Nani, you hear?'

Tantie Monica and Uncle Jamesie and the baby came up on the day before Christmas Eve. On that day we baked the Christmas cake and the bread, with the baby going from hand to hand.

On Christmas Eve we were up very early. Nobody wanted to miss one minute of the thrilling commotion that would begin before the sun was up and go on until late into the night. Children rushed from one exciting event to another. Sometimes we were torn between two or more attractions taking place at the same time: Tantie Monica putting down the bright new linoleum in the veranda; Ma and Uncle Leroy killing the pig down by the shed; Uncle Jamesie climbing on to the roof to nail down galvanize that was sticking up.

By six o'clock in the evening, most of the cooking had been overcome, and we were finally dressing up the drawing room. Then the children took their tea — some of the Christmas bread, with the first pieces from the ham that had been boiling all afternoon in the pitch-oil tin, and a cool cup of sorrel full of the smell of clove. On a night like this, Ma would not insist that we drink something hot to warm our chests before going to sleep.

After we had eaten and sat in the Morris chairs again to marvel at the beauty of our drawing room, we willingly went to our beds to give Father Christmas a chance to make his ghostly visit. We talked in low, excited voices in the darkened bedroom, the little ones on the bed and the big ones on bedding spread all over the floor. Carlyle and Anthony had to find a space on the bedroom floor, too, for their usual sleeping place, the drawing room, was out of bounds tonight. Out in the drawing room the big-people were opening the barrel from Mammy Patsy and talking in low voices as if they, too, were waiting for Father Christmas.

Then Uncle Leroy's friends began to fill up the gallery, wishing the house a Happy Christmas, talking rowdily all at the same time, and singing parang. Now that I was learning Spanish at school I could understand a little of what the Christmas songs meant, but parang was just as pretty whether or not the words made any sense. One of the party was strumming on a cuatro, some of them were beating spoons against bottles, and others shaking chac-chacs. After a while we could hear Pappy's voice in the gallery, leading the parang, and the fellas cheering him loudly at the end of each song. We could smell ham passing, and black cake, and glasses were clinking.

Before we fell asleep the company had drifted off noisily to another house, taking Uncle Leroy and Uncle Jamesie with them. Sometimes the two of them reached back home on Christmas morning, still singing.

And then Christmas was past and I had to start thinking about school again. Over the season everything to do with La Puerta had faded out of my mind. It was hard to believe that such a place as Mr Cephas's house existed. I had put away the Circus-horse, too, and even Anjanee! Poor Anjanee! Was she going to come back to school! What was happening to her, I wondered. What would become of Anjanee if she had to drop out of school?

I tried to believe that she was coming back. And I turned again to thinking of how I could persuade Ma not to send me back to my father. I began to look so miserable that Ma called me one day, to talk, I knew, about the reopening of school. We sat on the back steps together, with a big cocoa-basket full of peas to be shelled.

'So you want to live home,' she asked, as we tackled the peas.

'Yes, Ma,' I replied. She seemed to have softened a little, though I knew that Ma was not a person who changed her mind easily. She spoke in a kindly voice.

'You remember, Lacey, when you pass your exam to go to high school, and on top of that your father say he would mind you, how your Mammy was so glad! Because now she could save some money, so she could get to go to school, too. You remember?'

'Yes, Ma.'

'She never get the chance you have, you know. None of my children ever get a chance like that. Your Uncle Leroy was a bright, bright little fella in school. He wanted to be a aeroplane mechanic! You ever see that? And don't talk about your mother – she worse! You know what she wanted to be? A dentist!'

Ma looked at me with a proud smile creasing her eyes, and I had to smile, too, although I could tell that this conversation was leading me straight back into my father's house.

'When your Mammy was a little girl, small like Ruth and Charlene, your great-grandmother (God rest her soul) had some false teeth that was always falling down. The plate wouldn't stay on her gum for hell. So she was always cursing the dentist that give her the plate. She used to say she would find a good dentist that could give her teeth to stay in her mouth. But poor soul, she didn't have no money, so all she could do was curse the dentist behind his back. And Patsy used to hug her up and say, "Don't mind that, Mammy Christina, don't mind. When I get big I will 'come a dentist and stick back your teeth in your mouth for you."'

Ma was overcome with giggling, mostly in her bosom; then she sobered up again: 'But none of them get further than Balatier Government Primary School, bright as they was.'

She was silent for a while. She wanted me to

think. But I knew already that I would go back to Mr Cephas's house. I could not let my mother down.

'Your Mammy will have to drop out of school if your father stop minding you. And for he to mind you, he want you living there, so he could show off with his 'daughter'. He not helping you out of the goodness of his heart, you know. He just using you to puff up he chest!'

Now Ma was tearing open the pods in a most violent manner, wrenching out the peas and flinging them into the basin.

'Hm. Hm. As if he bring you where you reach. He don't know how you get food to eat, and shoes to walk the road to school all these years, and books to learn you lesson so you could come now and pass your exam! Now he doing like is he that see you through and put you in secondary school. But don't mind. Stay and eat all his food, let him put his hand in his pocket and feed you, clothe you and buy all those expensive schoolbooks, for I don't know where we would get the money.'

She was calmer now, as though she had finished tearing out Mr Cephas's guts with the last few pods she had shelled. She turned a wistful face to me: 'And we want to let Mammy Patsy get her chance, too, not so?'

Ma had sent a message for my father to come for me the Saturday before school reopened, at four o'clock. He arrived exactly on time and Ma invited him to come in. She had banished all children to the back yard. Pappy was taking a rest and Uncle Leroy was down in the kitchen packing a box of vegetables and eggs for me to take to town.

Ma told my father that she had given me bus fare to come home for Carnival. She pointed out, rather reproachfully, that it was natural for me to want to see my family. My father agreed wholeheartedly and nodded with all his might.

'How she behaving?' Ma asked.

'Good! Good! Very good!' he replied, again with much nodding.

'She helping in the house?'

'Yes, yes. Yes, Ma Willie.'

'All right,' said Ma. 'Well, I hope she ain't looking no thinner the next time I see her. Lacey, go and call Carlyle; and tell Leroy you ready to go.'

When Carlyle had loaded my belongings into the car, and Uncle Leroy had presented my father with the box of food, Ma allowed the children in, but only after they had washed their feet.

The children stood and scrutinized my father's clothes with awe, for, sitting in our drawing room, he looked like somebody who had just arrived from America. Pappy came out of the bedroom and my father sprang out of the chair to shake his hand.

'Mr Johnson, sir!' he said, then stepped back, all but saluting my grandfather.

Pappy peered at him as if trying to place him, while he made his way to his chair.

'Cephas!' he said, when he had seated himself comfortably.

'Yes, sir!'

'You come to take up the child?'

'Yes, Mr Johns ...'

'Well, you be sure to give due care and attention to our child, you understand? If any harm befall this child of ours, you shall answer for it. You have much to atone for ...'

'I know, sir ...'

'Fulfil your atonement with honour! Go in peace!'

My father was only too glad to take his leave.

Everybody followed me down to the car in a noisy procession, with dogs leaping around us and all the little children vying with each other to hold my hand. Just before I got into the car, Ma put her arms around me and rubbed my back. She didn't so much as look at Mr Cephas.

As fast as he could, Mr Cephas manoeuvred his car out of our rough, narrow Trace. He was gripping the wheel, and his jaw was set in a stony silence. When we finally got out on to the main road, he seemed to relax a little.

By the time we got to Junction, it was as though he felt he was out of Ma's sight and hearing. He loosened up. Then he began his speech.

It was first of all about Ungratefulness: Look at the opportunity I was getting to live in a decent home, a decent family, instead of that hole I had grown up in, that low-class hole, between all those coolie and ole-nigger; those backward people with no ambition; and half-naked children running about with no owner; none of them knew what a decent home was ... and so on.

Then it was about Disrespect: 'I am your father, and you have to respect me and obey me. Your grandmother and your mother teaching you to disrespect me. But I will show them — I will teach you to respect me! You think because you have a little more schooling than me that I is nobody and you could disrespect me. But you make a mistake. Everybody will see that my daughter with all her schooling have to respect me. You will behave yourself in my house!'

It was a very uncomfortable journey. I wanted to jump out of the car and run back home.

When we arrived at the house, Miss Velma was in her rocking chair in the gallery, with her head tied and her *Daily Word* on her lap. The scene looked very much the same as on the first day I arrived.

But things were not the same. Miss Velma was uncomfortable. She greeted me mournfully, as before, but at first she wouldn't look straight at me. When she turned her eyes on me, they were half pleading, half reproachful.

As my father slammed down my suitcase in the gallery and stalked back out to the car, I knew that this was going to be a fight to the finish.

A great deal of painting had taken place in Mr Cephas's house over the Christmas holidays, mainly on the outside. The drawing-room floor was now covered with a carpet deep as grass and the Christmas tree was still up. It was a huge one which almost touched the ceiling, and there were so many decorations on it that you could hardly see what kind of tree it was.

Before I could start unpacking, Miss Velma called me into the kitchen to have something to eat.

'You spend a nice Christmas?' she asked.

'Yes, thank you, Miss Velma.'

'Ours wasn't so nice,' Miss Velma said, and was silent for a while. She went and cut a piece of her Christmas cake to put on my plate. Then she sat at the table with me.

'Your daddy wasn't so pleased at how you didn't stay here for the Christmas. From the day you leave, he just holding his head in his hand. And to make it worse, when his friends come in the house they asking him where his daughter, and he don't know what to tell them.'

Miss Velma got up and shuffled over to the sink with my plate and cup. She continued to speak, with her back to me.

'You see, he boast so much about his daughter that now he don't know how to tell people he not really in charge of you. It spoil his whole Christmas. I never see him down in the dumps so, in a Christmas season.'

Michael now burst in through the kitchen door. He stopped in his tracks when he saw me, and a grin spread over his face.

'Lacey! You come back!' He stood looking shyly at me. Then his face changed, as though he'd suddenly remembered something. 'Coming just now,' he said. 'Going and bathe.' He darted out of the kitchen and soon we heard the shower running.

Miss Velma smiled sadly.

'That is who miss you the most!' she said. 'Every day he asking: "When Lacey coming back? Mammy, Lacey not coming back? Mammy, I could go and spend a day by Lacey?"'

She lowered her voice. 'Poor child. The father ready to give him away, because you know he not doing so good in school. But your father so proud of you! He want you to go to University and study to be a doctor or a lawyer. That is the hopes he had for Michael; but he give up on him. Michael never get a good report like yours. He ...'

The shower stopped, so Miss Velma changed the topic. She asked how my grandmother was, and 'all the others'.

Miss Velma was always very vague about my family. She knew about Ma, but after Ma it was 'all the others'. It was as though she pictured my family as a horde of people out in the Balatier bush whom nobody could count or put names to.

Michael hurried back into the kitchen after what was a very brief bath. He was still pulling a jersey down over his head, and when it was on, it was both back-to-front and inside-out. That was of no concern to him. He had come to drag me from the kitchen, to show me what he had got for Christmas.

There were toy vehicles already missing their wheels; some guns; games that didn't interest him because they were too difficult. He dug through all this to find a storybook that his godmother had given him for Christmas. He begged me to read it for him.

I read him one story and then I turned to unpacking. He talked without stopping, and was still talking to me when I got into bed and drifted off to sleep.

The next morning Miss Velma dressed and left for church without looking in on me. Normally she would check to see whether I wanted to go with her.

When I got to school on the first day, the classroom was full of chattering children. I looked around for Anjanee but she wasn't there.

The bell rang and we went down to assembly. It was a long assembly because the principal gave a speech that she called 'a refresher course on the rules of La Puerta Government Secondary School'. When she talked about staying away from the Plaza, Doreen Sandiford and her gang rolled their eyes at each other.

Assembly lasted for almost the whole of the first period, and as usual, students took as long as they possibly could to file back to their classrooms. By the time we finally settled down for roll call, the second period had begun, and there was still no sign of Anjanee.

In class I drew pictures in my book and kept glancing at the door. I was restless, and anxious, unable to pay any attention to the lesson.

By break time I had given up. Anjanee was not coming. Now it was quite impossible to settle down to schoolwork. For the rest of the day I read a storybook placed on my lap, or scribbled and drew all over the covers of my notebooks. In Mrs Lopez's class I put my head down on the desk and slept.

The next day was the same. Anjanee did not turn up, and I was like a haunted person. I cut Mr Tewarie's class. I went and sat behind the music room, staring into space and thinking how I would like to see Mr Cephas dead.

I pictured a car accident, with his car so mashed up that you couldn't tell the front from the back. Or he could die from some sickness. He could get a stroke and drop down dead in his office.

Suppose one day I was sitting in class and the principal sent for me, to give me the message that my father was dead! . . .

Terrible things could happen to you if you called misfortune down on other people, Ma always said to us. The misfortune could fall on you instead. So I took my mind off Mr Cephas and thought about home.

I was going home on the Friday before Carnival. I would have four whole days in Balatier. That brightened me up a little. We would go to see the bands in Junction. And Ma usually kept us home from school on Ash Wednesday because, she said, she wasn't putting us on the road when there were still fellas all about stale-drunk from Carnival. I wondered if she would let me stay home on Ash Wednesday.

But, then, Carnival was seven weeks away! And afterwards, I would have to come back to Mr Cephas's house for the rest of the term. It suddenly struck me: I would have to live in Mr Cephas's house for the rest of my years at school! Until I'd finished all my exams!

That was too much to think about, so I got up and started to make my way back to the classroom for the next period.

Another day came and Anjanee still did not turn up. At lunchtime Doreen Sandiford called me to sit with her gang. They always had lunch at the teacher's desk in our classroom. I was something of a celebrity to them, because, they said, I didn't *forget* to give Ma Lopez pound for pound.

I ate lunch with them for the rest of the week.

The following Monday, Anjanee returned. She slid through the door like a ghost, her face thinner and paler than I remembered. It was halfway through the first period, and since I could never get Anjanee to talk in class, I had to wait until break time.

'What happen to you last week?' I asked impatiently when the bell rang.

'I was sick, and the baby was sick.' She sighed and put her head down on the desk. 'The baby get sick, so me and my mother carry him to the clinic. When the doctor see me, she say I looking more sick than the baby. She say I have anaemia.

'Anaemia? People doesn't stay home for that. Miss Velma tell me she have anaemia, and she does just take pills for it – she ain't so sick. The doctor tell you to stay home?'

'No.' She paused.

'You didn't have money?'

'Yes, I had money. I went and sell in the market every day in the holidays to get money to come to school. I was well ready for school ... but I had to stay and help my mother mind the baby until he get better.' Then she added, as if to protect her mother: 'She ain't have nobody else to help her.'

'And me,' I said, fiercely, 'I right back in my father house!'

Anjanee lifted her head and without speaking showed so much sympathy for me that I felt guilty.

'I will tell you lunchtime,' I promised. 'Let's go and drink some water and walk about a little bit, na!'

'You go ahead, Lacey. I ... not feeling for water.'

We ate our lunch in our usual spot on the far side of the playing field.

Anjanee listened gravely to my story, then she sighed. 'Well, Lacey,' she said. 'You will have to do that for your mother. Just stay there for now. It wouldn't kill you. Then when you pass your exam, and your mother pass her exam, too, allyu wouldn't have to worry again!'

She was peering into my face as if she thought I would disagree.

'I know, I know,' I said. 'I only staying there for my mother sake. If it wasn't for my mother ... I woulda do something to make them put me back home. *Some*thing. I don't know what, but *some*thing.'

Anjanee did not look any better as the days went by. She was so thin now that Marlon Peters began to call us Fatso and Thinso. Next to Anjanee, anybody in the world could seem fat.

It was not long before she started to miss days of school again, and once more she was badly out of her depth in every subject.

She was eating less and less. Out on our log she would sit with her lunch almost untouched on her lap and talk in a despairing tone.

'I have so much work to do home that every night I going to sleep tired and in the morning I waking up more tired. Sometimes I can't finish my work in time to get ready for school, because I so tired I can't move fast. Sun does come up and catch me still in my home clothes, and that time it don't make sense coming out. I would reach here mid-day!'

'So your brothers don't do *nothing* at all? They can't help your mother, too?' I asked. 'They should have my grandmother to deal with!'

'Them? Help? They can't even wash a kerchief! I washing their clothes since I eight years old!'

She stared ahead of her and was quiet for some time. Then she said, in a defeated voice: 'You know,

Lacey, I seeing myself just washing clothes, cooking food, sweeping house – all the time, for the rest of my life – just like my mother. I not going to pass my exam. I not even going to make the five years to the exam!'

'Anjanee, I tell you already: let us stay and study after school! I ain't care what Cephas say ...'

'No, Lacey, I don't want you to get in trouble!'

'Well, why we don't cut Tewarie class? You think he want to know if we there or not? He don't care!'

She shook her head violently. 'No, Lacey, we not cutting no class!'

'Okay, Miss Holy Mary. You go ahead. I cutting Tewarie class *today*. You could go and sit down in front of he – see if you learn anything!'

This threw her into a terrible state. She begged me not to do anything to get myself into trouble.

'Lacey, you will fail your exam! Or they might expel you for cutting classes!' She pleaded with me. 'Lacey, behave yourself, na!'

On afternoons I drifted home by a long, roundabout route. Sometimes I walked with Anjanee to the bus station, and we stood and talked inside the waiting area. It did not matter to me whether Mr Cephas saw me down there again, but Anjanee was very concerned and insisted that we go inside.

On some days, instead of going straight home after school, I headed in the opposite direction: I made my way over to Ma Zelline's house. Tall razor grass jostled with the dasheen bush and ratchet in her front yard. The dasheen bush was parting the razor grass with its enormous dark leaves, and the ratchet stood upright with its many hands fighting off grass and vine. The door and the windows of her house were tightly shut. Still, I paused in front of her gate, or walked slowly past, as if I thought that her scandalous cackle would come floating out from somewhere inside.

When one day I walked to the bus station with Anjanee and waited with her for the bus, and then on top of that went to look at Ma Zelline's house, I reached home at a dangerous hour. Miss Velma greeted me with a 'Hm!' She wore her mournful expression all the time now, and although she was never unkind to me, when she spoke to me it was in a grumbling voice. At the same time she had an air, I thought, of someone who was slyly hoping for trouble. It was as though she was waiting for some great calamity that would allow her to band her belly, hold her head, and bawl.

'Hm!' she said, without sounding too vexed. 'What you will say to your father when he catch you out in the road this hour?'

Mr Cephas and I had very little to say to each other. Every so often he would sit in the drawing room and lecture loudly about Ungrateful Children. Yet he still tried, now and then, to start up a friendly conversation with me.

'Your old man still betting on you to come first in test, you know! Don't let down me and your Auntie V!'

Mostly, however, he watched me like a dangerous prisoner, out of the corner of his eye. He, too, seemed to be waiting for something unpleasant to happen, something of my doing.

He was still in the habit of going through my

schoolbooks, searching for high marks and words of praise from teachers. Sometimes, therefore, I did my homework at school and left all my exercise books in my locker so that he would have nothing to gloat over.

Whenever Anjanee did not come to school, I stayed in the classroom at lunchtime and ate with Doreen Sandiford's gang. On some days they would disappear as soon as the afternoon roll had been called, and only reappear at the end of the day.

I began moving out with them. It was as though the whole school belonged to us. They knew every nook and cranny of the buildings and grounds, and we settled in a different hiding place each time: between the lockers; in empty classrooms; behind a wall of hibiscus that seemed to grow wild and untended just a few yards from the home-ec room.

It was not only Spanish classes that we were skipping. We cut geography, history . . . even maths.

Doreen had a little spindly cousin in our class who had to report to us at the end of every day and tell us what homework the teachers had given. But I soon began to have difficulties with the assignments because of all the classwork I was missing. (Doreen just made the little cousin do hers for her when she couldn't.) I would scribble down something and hand it up, but sometimes I did not bother.

I certainly did not bother myself doing any Spanish homework, for Mr Tewarie only occasionally made a fuss over work not done. Every now and then he would rant and rave because out of the thirty-five of us, only five or six handed in his assignment. But on other days he did not even remember to take up the work that he had given.

My marks fell right down. But, I thought, I would just learn up everything in time for midterm test, so that the teachers would have good marks to put in my report book again. Yet it would serve Mr Cephas right if I got a bad report. How cut up he would be if I were to fail at everything!

But then, right after midterm test was Carnival, and I was going home for Carnival, so failing the test was out of the question. I had to have good marks to take home.

There was still time, though. I decided I would lime with Doreen Sandiford and the others for one or two more weeks, and then I would start to take on the midterm test.

One day at lunchtime I noticed that Doreen's friends were moving more swiftly than usual towards the front of the classroom. Anjanee was absent, so I was going to have lunch with them. Now they stood in a close knot by the desk, talking in low voices, and when I joined them I realized that they were counting money.

'Where allyu get that!' I asked in alarm, and backed away. This gang of brazen girls could do anything, even break in somewhere and take money. Janice caught my sleeve and pulled me back.

'Hush,' she said in a dramatic whisper. 'We going in the Plaza for chicken-and-chips. Put what you have.'

'I don't have no money,' I said, and started to move off, but Doreen Sandiford took me by the arm.

'Na. She could come,' she said to the others. 'We have enough. Let's go.'

So I was on my way to the Plaza, breaking the strictest rule of La Puerta Government Secondary School – putting God out of my thoughts, as Ma would say.

And immediately I began to struggle to put Ma out of my thoughts, for if we were caught . . . !

I had been to the Plaza several times, with Miss Velma, and with Uncle Leroy. When we came to town to sell the cocoa, Uncle Leroy would take Carlyle and me into the Plaza and buy us a hot dog and soft drink. Then we walked around admiring the bright store windows before we took the bus home. Ma said she would not put her foot in there because it was not a place for poor people.

The Plaza was only about ten minutes' walk from the school if you went out the front gate and took the main road. But Doreen Sandiford's gang made their way around the playing field behind the school and squeezed through a break in the fence. Then we hustled through a maze of back streets.

Once we were inside, we felt safe. The corridors were so crowded and busy that it did not seem likely that anyone would notice a few girls in La Puerta Government Sec uniform. One of the hottest calypsos of the Carnival season was coming out of the piped music system, following us wherever we went:

> I go break-out
> I go break-away.
> I go break-out

I go break-away.
When you hear the shout
What they talking bout?
Me that break-out
Me that break-away.

Soon we were brazenly singing along with it and dancing our way from one store window to the next.

We were inspecting the clothes on display, each of us pretending to the others that we were allowed to go to Carnival *fêtes* and that we were looking for an outfit to wear to the next *fête*. Nobody saw Mr Tewarie until he shouted at us from the doorway of Ponderosa Wild West Bar and Saloon: 'Ey! What is this? What going on here? ...'

Nobody waited to hear any more. The whole group turned and stampeded through the Plaza, running wildly until we were outside and safe in a back street.

Then Doreen Sandiford stopped and faced us, her arms akimbo. 'So wait. Allyu 'fraid Tewarie now? What happen to the chicken-and-chips?'

Not many of us were in favour of going back into the Plaza now for anything on earth, but Doreen Sandiford sucked her teeth and headed back up the road. Two others decided to go with her. The rest of us debated whether we should wait there, go back to school, or go back into the Plaza with the others. Whatever we did, we were in trouble already. We decided to stay where we were but to keep a sharp lookout all the while.

They returned eventually with the boxes of chicken and chips. Swiftly we made our way through the back streets again. We squeezed through the fence and hid behind a clump of bushes on the edge of the playing field. There we divided up the food and swallowed it almost whole ('Just how *macajuel* snake does eat,' Ma would say).

The bell rang. We did not know what to expect when we turned up for roll call. What was clear was that we should not be late for roll call. Doreen Sandiford assured us that Tewarie was probably drunk and couldn't identify us, so we needn't worry.

We slid into our seats for roll call before Miss Hafeez arrived. She looked as calm and pleasant as always. She called the roll, made some announcements, and left. We, the Plaza gang, winked at each other in triumph.

I did not cut any classes that afternoon. In fact, I vowed that I would now begin to prepare for the midterm test – no more playing the fool. It was one thing to spite Mr Cephas, but I still had Ma to face, and my uncles, and Pappy, and Mammy Patsy.

The next morning, however, before she called roll, Miss Hafeez read out a list of names – the whole of Doreen Sandiford's gang, and me – and told us to go down to the conference room. We were caught.

Miss Hafeez came to us in the conference room and spoke to us briefly before she went to her first class. Looking very disappointed, and hurt, she told us that we were going to be suspended for a week. She instructed us to go and sit outside the principal's office and wait for a letter to take home. We would have to return with a parent or guardian to talk with the principal, and then go home again.

I was dazed. Ma prided herself on the fact that she had never yet been summoned into a school to answer for misbehaviour from any child of hers. She warned us that the first child to bring such shame on her old head would be the one to send her to her grave. What was I going to do?

We walked down to the principal's office with our hearts in our mouths. We sat waiting in silence until Doreen Sandiford said, in a matter-of-fact voice: 'My father going to kill me with licks.'

Some of the girls burst into tears. Doreen Sandiford

continued to talk to herself. 'They send for my parents when I was in primary school, and I carry the letter for my mother. She give me two slaps, but she say if I promise to behave myself she wouldn't tell my father. Then she say if anything so happen again, she telling him one time. So now my tail in fire.'

I had to work out what I was going to do. The letter would be addressed to Ma. I would have to use the bus fare Ma had given me to come home for Carnival to go and deliver a summons to her instead! That was unthinkable. I would rather die.

Now I wished that we had put down Mr Cephas as my guardian when we came to register. How could I take such a letter to Ma?

The solution was to have them address the letter to my father. He could do anything he pleased – go into a rage, shout, hit me with a book – as long as Ma didn't find out about this. But ... he might send the news to my family. He might send a message right away, just for spite – just to upset Ma. No, I would have to take the letter to Miss Velma. She might be too frightened to let him know.

It slowly dawned on me, however, that suspension meant *staying home! not being allowed to go to school!* He was bound to find out! But no, Mr Cephas left early on mornings, before I was ready for school, and I was supposed to be home before him. I would just have to do some writing in my exercise books each day, for when he inspected them.

The secretary called us up one by one to give us our letters. When it was my turn, I told her that I was living with my father and stepmother in La

Puerta now – Mr and Mrs Cephas – and that my grandmother was too old and sick to come all the way up from Balatier.

She looked at me out of the corner of her eye. 'You sure you not trying something?'

'No, miss. Look on my form and you will see my father name: Orville Cephas.'

She scrutinized the form and then said: 'Okay, so send it to Mr and Mrs Orville Cephas, then?'

When Miss Velma finally opened the letter and read it, she sat down heavily and fanned herself. At first she was not going to open the letter because Mr Cephas's name was on it. I had to tell her what it was about in order to persuade her to open it before Mr Cephas could see it. Now she was looking as though the Great Calamity had arrived at last.

She whispered: 'Why you leave the school and go up there, child?'

'Some children was going for chicken-and-chips, and they ...'

'Chicken-and-chips? You went for chicken-and-chips? I didn't give you lunch from home? What happen to your lunch?'

'Nothing, Miss Velma.'

'Then why you have to leave the school and go for chicken-and-chips? You want your father to say that I ain't give you no lunch? Eh, child? You want your father to vex with me?'

'No, Miss Velma.'

She started to fan herself again. 'Child, why you bring this trouble on people? What going to happen when your father come home? Jesus Lord, deliver us!...'

'You going to tell my father, Miss Velma?'

She stopped fanning and peered at me. 'How you mean? And your father have to go and see the principal?'

'*You* could go, Miss Velma. The teacher say to bring a parent or guardian. They didn't say you must bring your father.'

Miss Velma spent a long time studying her hands in her lap, turning them this way and that. I could see from her face that all kinds of things were going on inside her head.

Then she rose, sighing, from the chair.

'I will have to put on my clothes,' she said.

Miss Velma sat wringing her hands while we waited to see the principal. Sometimes she muttered to herself. Then she sent me a long, reproachful glance and rearranged herself on the chair. She sat now with her lips pursed, firmly holding her handbag on her lap.

After some time the vice-principal passed through the lobby and stopped to find out what we were there for. Miss Velma handed him the letter. He scribbled rapidly on it, gave it back to her, and continued on his way.

We sat still waiting for a few moments until we realized that we had been dismissed. We made our way home, with Miss Velma walking so briskly that I had some trouble keeping up with her.

The rest of the day I moved around beside Miss Velma, helping with the housework; but her lips remained tightly pursed, and she seemed not to notice me at all. Michael came home, was fed, and disappeared again.

When Mr Cephas came home, Miss Velma was resting in her room. She hurried out and served him his food. Then he, too, disappeared again.

The next day was even more uncomfortable. Miss Velma was on tenterhooks. At the sound of a passing car she would stop whatever she was doing and wait anxiously for a few moments. Every now and then she went into the drawing room and moved aside the curtains to peep outside.

On the third day she (and I) came near to suffering a heart attack. Mr Cephas's car drew up at lunchtime. He was stamping through the house before we could even brace ourselves. Miss Velma was in the back yard washing. Mr Cephas came upon me as I was in the kitchen, mixing juice.

He stood and glared at me.

'So tell me what it is going on here, miss? You get suspend from school and I don't even know! Eh! I had to hear it from outside? Where your stepmother? Velma!'

Miss Velma was already fumbling with the half-door latch.

'What it is happening here, Velma – you know this child on suspension? What it is she tell you – she playing sick?'

'No, Cephas, I know she on suspension . . .'

'*What!* So how I don't know, and I is the one feeding and clothing her and sending her to school? How I don't know, I is the dog? Everybody in the world know my daughter get in trouble, my wife and all know, and I don't know! I had to hear it from some young fella in my workplace who have a sister in the school! That is how I find out! Something going on around here, man – the two of you in *complot* against me? Eh? Allyu plan for me? Allyu take a big man to make a fool?'

161

Miss Velma had come inside and closed the half door behind her. She seemed to take a deep breath. Her mouth trembled for a moment, but then she began to speak, in a soft but determined voice.

'Cephas,' she said. '*You* bring your daughter here. You don't know the child, the child don't know you. But you want your daughter to come and live by you. So you bring her. And what satisfaction you get out of that? All you get is trouble. This child should go back where she belong before you really get something you didn't bargain for.'

Miss Velma had stepped out of her half-dead, frightened self. She had finished speaking and Mr Cephas was still standing looking at her with his mouth open.

'Oho,' he said, finally. 'So now you want to tell me what I must do and what I mustn't do. First allyu ganging up against me to cover up what going on in my own house; and now you giving me orders. But no! None of you will give me orders! I is the man in this house! I is the man! I is the man!'

Miss Velma stood her ground without a word. Mr Cephas turned to me abruptly: 'So you going to tell me what happen? What kind of shame is this you bringing on me, eh?'

I didn't know what to say to him. The silence was too much for Miss Velma now, and she told him what had happened.

'And so you take up yourself and go down there to answer for this little ... You have no right! That is a disgrace to my name! Let her grandmother go and answer for her. They ain't teach her no behaviour, let them go and take the shame. You stay out of it! When she misbehave, let her go for her grandmother!'

He ranted some more, then turned and marched back out through the drawing room. We heard his car start up and drive away.

A few moments passed before Miss Velma seemed to shake herself out of a dream. She pulled a chair and sat down.

'You want some juice, Miss Velma?' I was already getting out the glass and ice.

'Yes, child,' she said to herself. 'Give me some juice.'

When I turned around with the glass of juice, she was sitting with her head propped on her elbows, massaging her forehead.

'Child,' she groaned, 'you cause enough trouble. I not against you, but I don't want you here. Better you go back. You turning your father into a worse beast than he was to begin with . . .'

Miss Velma stopped herself, then got up, shaking her head, to go back to her washing.

Many times that week I woke up in the night with a start, because I thought Mammy Patsy was standing over my bed, looking down at me with Miss Velma's sorrowful face.

The suspended students came back out to school just two days before the midterm test.

Anjanee was not at school on that day, and I was relieved. I did not look forward to seeing her. When she came to school on the following day, she could hardly even talk to me without sounding as if she would cry.

'Lacey, you don't care nothing?' was all she ever said about the suspension. For the whole day it lay like a heavy stone between us. Anjanee seemed to be gazing at me reproachfully, out of an older person's eyes.

I felt as if I was going around spoiling everything. I had made an enemy of Miss Velma, and now I had let Anjanee down so badly that it did not seem she would ever recover. She was struggling so hard to come to school, and I was throwing it all away.

Then sooner or later my family would find out about the suspension, and my cutting classes, and the low marks I was getting . . .

I went into the midterm test with the same panic that Anjanee felt at every test. I had missed more classes than she! There was no help I could offer her, for I had missed so much since the beginning of term that I did not even know where the class had reached.

The first test was geography. I read through the question paper and my head began to spin. It was all gibberish to me! I did not know anything – I had even forgotten things I knew before. I was not much better off at maths, or Spanish or any of the other subjects. I sat and wrote what I could, but I knew that I had failed miserably.

Then right after the midterm test I would be going home for Carnival, and I would have nothing good to show my family. At Christmas I had taken home all my test papers, and everyone was so proud that Uncle Leroy had sent them to my mother, so that she would not be left out. Uncle Leroy was expecting me to bring my midterm test papers when I came home at Carnival.

'Well, you know is only high marks you could make now, Miss Lady,' he had said to me. 'You can't go and make no Duck, because we can't send that for your Mammy Patsy. The Post Office don't handle poultry.'

Now I couldn't even smile at his joke. He would have nothing funny to say about these marks. Uncle Leroy was full of jokes, but he could get very sour with us for 'playing the jackass' with school.

Once he caught Carlyle roaming in Junction with a group of friends during school hours. There and then he made Carlyle take off his shoes and hand them over. Carlyle had to walk to school barefoot for days, and in the end it was Ma who begged Uncle Leroy to give him back his shoes.

What were they going to say about my schoolwork? As for the suspension! … I felt that Ma would just look at me and know the whole story. Nobody would have to tell her anything.

I could not go home at Carnival. I decided to write to Ma, saying that I would save the bus fare and not bother to come home until the end of term.

The school's Carnival Frolic was on Friday afternoon. Marlon Peters's gang was bringing out a band called 'Tails of the Meek Heroes.' The characters in the band were Ketch-Tail, Cut-Tail, Pissing-Tail, Haul-Your-Tail, Tail-Between-Your-Legs, Planasse-Tail, and others. Charmaine Springer was entering the calypso competition. Her calypso name was Lady Reporter, and she had made up a calypso called 'The Teacher Don't Know Me'.

I didn't stay for the Frolic.

On Carnival Monday and Tuesday, whenever the wind blew towards us from Main Street it brought snatches of music. But our part of town was very quiet, and I did not go out at all.

Mr Cephas had left the house with a group of very merry cronies on the Sunday night, and only reappeared on Monday after the Jouvert was over at about eleven o'clock, to bathe and eat before he plunged back into the town. Miss Velma sent Michael to see the bands pass down Main Street, warning him to be back before dark. She stayed at home, and so did I, she in her room and I in mine.

By the time we came back out to school on Ash Wednesday, Anjanee had softened again. She was more worried about me than reproachful. Her one concern was that I catch up on my schoolwork and begin to make good marks again.

On mornings she would ask anxiously: 'Lacey, you do the homework?' and she would smile with relief when I took out my exercise books and showed her all my homework done. She did not let me out of her sight all day, following me everywhere, as tired as she was, to make sure that I did not slip away and hide instead of coming to class.

But she was the one to worry about. She did not look at all well. Even her school shirt was wearing thin. It was no longer yellow: the colour now was nearer to cream, and holes were beginning to appear in it. Like the shirt, Anjanee was beginning to seem very pale, even transparent. It was as if she was fading away.

Sometimes her voice was almost a whisper, and her movements were slow and weary. In class she propped her head on her elbow and fell asleep. When we had P.E. the teacher didn't press her to take part in the games and exercises. She let her sit and watch.

One day Anjanee didn't even open her lunch.

'What happen, Anjanee, you not eating today?' I asked with some alarm, because she looked so worn out that I thought she could topple off the log at any minute.

'No – I not feeling hungry. I will eat it later.'

I searched her face. 'You taking the pills the doctor give you?'

'Yes, I taking the pills.'

'Well, they not helping you? You not getting better?'

Anjanee bowed her head. She spoke as if musing to herself: 'The doctor say I have to rest, too. But how I will rest? I have to help my mother. And I want to come to school. I want to come to school and pass my exam!' She had begun to speak fiercely. 'And if I can't come to school and pass my exam ...!' She stopped, staring out across the playing field, where there was nothing to be seen.

One Monday morning Anjanee fainted in assembly. She just sank to the floor next to me, without a sound. It took a few seconds before everyone was aware of what had happened. I was kneeling on the floor trying to pick her up when some teachers rushed over to us. They drew me away and a teacher lifted her up in one scoop. As he hurried away with her dangling body, I tried to follow, but Miss Hafeez put her arm around my shoulders and made me stay.

Anjanee didn't come to school the next day. That was not surprising, and yet I drooped for the whole morning, and then in the afternoon I went and sat behind the music room, feeling tense and uneasy.

For three days Anjanee did not appear. On Friday morning I woke up with such a heavy feeling that I could not move. A weight like lead seemed to be pressing down on me. My head and all my limbs felt like board, and right in the centre, just above my navel, was a tight knot that was going to stifle me.

It was the dream I had had the night before. Mammy Patsy was sitting in class next to me in Anjanee's thin, faded shirt. But the Circus-horse barked something at her, and then her seat was empty.

At another moment Mammy Patsy was standing in the middle of Miss Velma's dasheen patch, calling to me to bring her my geography book; but I had thrown the geography book in the dustbin at school. Then I was running down the road towards the school to get the geography book, running through all the back streets of La Puerta, turning corners right and left, but getting no nearer to the school. So I went back to where I had left Mammy Patsy. But when I got there it was Ma Zelline in the dasheen patch, and she threw one reproachful glance at me and fell down dead from a stroke.

The heaviness remained. In fact, it grew worse as I got ready for school. I moved so slowly that Miss Velma asked me whether I was sick. I replied that I was okay, but she continued to eye me as though she could see some trouble.

As I walked to school that Friday, I thought of all the time I had wasted over the past weeks. I would have to settle down and get serious. I had to make sure that I had a good report at the end of the term to send to my mother.

I sat in Mrs Lopez's class trying to concentrate on mathematics, but I could not. Anjanee had now missed a whole week of school. Was she too sick to come to school? Or had she really given up? She *had* to come back to school, she just *had* to come back!

Then I heard the Circus-horse angrily calling my name, and I suddenly realized that everybody was busy writing something while I sat and stared straight ahead of me.

'You! Madam! What is going on? No Miss Jugmo-hansingh, eh? Well, if you can't live without your sidekick, then you can go and join her wherever she is, if that is all the ambition you have. Now you just as badly off as she, anyway. When you play with dog, you get fleas.'

I sprang to my feet in such a rage that my chair fell over with a terrible crash. 'Your *mother* must be the dog! Your *mother* ...!'

I couldn't believe that this was my voice, shouting

these words at a teacher! This was absolutely the rudest thing I had ever done in the whole of my life.

So once more I was sitting outside the principal's office, waiting for a letter to take home. I had a pain in my belly and couldn't think straight. This time I would have to take the letter to Mr Cephas, for Miss Velma was not going to stick her neck out for me again.

Mr Cephas? Not Mr Cephas. He had washed his hands of me. He had made it clear that if I got myself into trouble at school again, it would be Ma's business! Ma would have to be summoned to come into the school because of me!

The secretary called me and gave me the letter.

Then I had to go back to the classroom for my books.

As I walked away, I was thinking about how Ma would have to put on her going-out clothes to come into the school and hear about all my misdeeds: the Plaza, the suspension, cutting classes, not studying ... And now I had *cursed a teacher's mother*! All of this they would pile on her head.

It would be very easy if she would just give me a licking. That would be a relief. But she probably would not lift a finger at me. She would just be sad, and hurt, and ashamed. And Pappy would have to hear about it, too, and Uncle Leroy, and my mother working herself to death for us up in New York.

As I climbed the steps I realized that there was one big commotion going on upstairs. The whole floor was alive with excitement. Children were talking at the tops of their voices and darting in and out of classroom doors.

My class was on its feet, except for two girls crying at their desks and Marlon Peters glued to his chair, thunderstruck. Everybody else was moving crazily about and all talking at the same time.

I didn't know that I had caused such a stir. What I had said to Mrs Lopez was so outrageous that it had shaken up almost the whole school! Then what would it do to Ma! She would get a stroke right away!

But nobody even noticed me. I was standing in the doorway and nobody was seeing me. So this couldn't be anything to do with me.

Yet I was suddenly cold with fright, and I wanted to rush back out before I could hear what it was that had everybody in such a state of shock.

Now everyone fell quiet. They stared at me speechlessly for a few seconds, then a girl came to me and said: 'Lacey! You ain't hear what happen? Anjanee drink poison!'

I grabbed my books and rushed out. I didn't want to hear the rest. I knew. She was dead. I made my way blindly down the stairs. The whole school was buzzing now, and I walked faster and faster – to the gate and out into the road.

I was crossing streets, turning corners, weaving my way through traffic. The belly pain was much worse, and now my insides seemed to have turned to liquid.

I found myself approaching the bus station. What I planned to do there, I didn't know. Take a bus home? But Ma would be so ashamed, and hurt, and so heartbroken that she might have to go and lie down and we would have to fan her, and she mightn't recover. And Mammy Patsy would have to give up night school and come home . . .

The dream of the night before was following me: I had let everybody down, and now what Anjanee had done to herself was my fault! She must have done it because I let her down!

I made an about-turn and shot back up the road. I had to stop thinking or my head would burst.

When I was a good distance from the bus station, I slowed down. It was still early, not even lunchtime. Miss Velma would ask why I was home so early. I would tell her I had belly pains. I would ask her for a tablet.

Miss Velma had all kinds of tablets – for her high blood pressure and her anaemia; for headache, for arthritis; for Mr Cephas's gallstones and Michael's worm-fits. She kept them somewhere in her bed-room so that Michael could not interfere with them.

I started to walk fast again. I would get tablets from Miss Velma. I had to stop thinking.

Miss Velma did not seem very surprised to see me. Somehow she had already heard the news of Anjanee and thought that the whole school had been sent home for the day.

'But what a thing, eh? These Indian girls so quick to take poison. You didn't know the girl – you know her?'

'No,' I said. 'I didn't know her.' Then I asked if I could have something for belly pains.

'Eh-eh! Like you drink some of what the girl drink!' Miss Velma chuckled. She was quite taken up with the news, even a little excited. Then she got serious. 'Since morning I could see something happen to you, you know. What kind of bellyache is this, now? Come.'

I followed her into the bedroom. She pulled a chair to the wardrobe and climbed on to the chair. She rummaged on top of the wardrobe for a while and then took down a shoe box.

It was crammed full of little bottles, boxes, envelopes, and tubes, all helter-skelter. She sat on the bed with the box on her lap and eyed me for a moment: 'Tell me what it is – you turn a Young Lady?'

I was only half listening, for I was looking into the box and thinking that there must be medicine in there for every pain in the world . . .

'All right,' Miss Velma was saying. 'I will give you

something for the belly pain, and then you will go and bathe.'

Miss Velma took out a bottle of yellowish liquid. She put back her medicine box in its place and led me to the kitchen. There I swallowed two large spoonfuls of the medicine without even tasting it.

'Go and bathe now,' Miss Velma ordered.

I nodded and went into my bedroom, where I sat down heavily on the bed. I was tired. Thoughts were racing around inside my head, but I didn't want to think too much. Anjanee – *dead?* I suddenly felt like screaming and I had to put my hand over my mouth. I didn't want Miss Velma to come rushing in.

Sooner or later she would go outside to take the clothes off the line, or clean fish, or tend her flowers. She spent a lot of time in the yard when Mr Cephas wasn't at home. As soon as she went outside, I would quickly find the box of medicine and take it into the bathroom with me.

I heard her calling.

'Yes, Miss Velma,' I called back. 'I going to bathe just now. I cooling off.'

'All right. I just going down by the market to come back.'

Then I heard her approaching and bent down to take off my shoes and socks. She stuck her head in the door and said, in a dramatic whisper, as if the two of us were in a plot together: 'I put something in the bathroom cupboard, in case. You know how to fix yourself up – in case?'

I nodded, and she left. As soon as I heard the front door close, I got up to go for the medicine box. I turned around to take my slippers from under the bed, and there, where I had been sitting, was a bright pink stain. Miss Velma was right!

For a brief moment I was very excited. I couldn't wait to tell Anjanee! Now we were both grown-up Young Ladies, I would announce to her as soon as ... But Anjanee wasn't there! Anjanee was not there for me to tell her anything, in my whole life, ever again! I put my hands to my ears and squeezed them tight against my head: 'No! Not true!' I shouted.

I sat down heavily. Something frightful was happening inside my head – a pounding, pounding, and a giddying tightness. For a moment I could not remember what to do next. Too many things were beating about in my head. Anjanee saying, 'Lacey, you don't care nothing?' The new suspension letter that I had in my notebook to take home to my family; and how Ma would have to put on her clothes and come up to La Puerta, and they would give her a seat and make her listen as they told of all the things I had done. My head was going to burst. I had to stop thinking.

I shot up. The medicine. I had to get some medicine. I rushed into the bedroom and dragged the chair to the wardrobe. The top of the wardrobe was piled high with all kinds of things, and I brought down a shower of old papers before I could find the shoebox.

I jumped off the chair to gather up the papers scattered on the floor. I was scooping up dusty, tattered newspapers, receipts, Christmas cards, photographs, and letters, and suddenly there in the pile was a picture of Miss Velma in her high-school uniform.

My head was getting bigger and bigger all the

time, stretching and stretching like a balloon ...
Now it was Anjanee's eyes looking at me reproachfully out of the photograph, and I knew what she
wanted to say to me ... My head now seemed to
burst into pieces, and I started to scream ... I
screamed until I didn't have to think anymore, when
everything went dark.

It was not until the Easter holidays that I started to go out into the yard again. I had spent weeks indoors.

After I came home from the hospital, I stayed in the bedroom day and night. I lay on the bed staring up at the underside of the roof for hours. What I was really doing was making my way across the room by travelling up and down the tracks in the galvanize.

This was a very difficult task, and it needed a great deal of time and patience. The galvanize was like the big garden: long beds lying side by side with canals in between. I had to walk the full length of every single bed and every single canal in order to get from one side of the room to the other. I had to cover the whole area – I could not miss a track. This took hours, for if you were not careful, you could easily slip off the track and end up in the wrong one, and forget where you had reached. Every time this happened I had to start all over again – up the first track, down the next, up the next one. . .

Nobody could get me out of the bedroom. I hardly ate anything and I did not talk.

At first, Ruth and Kenwyn would come to the door and stare, wide-eyed, at me. When night fell, they tiptoed into the room and curled up beside me on the bed.

Then they started coming into the room to chat, sometimes to tell me long stories of the dogs, or the pigs. At night they talked to me until they fell asleep – they did not seem to notice that I was not answering. To them it was just as before, when we lay on the big bed together every night and talked until we were too tired to say another word.

On some nights Ma came and lay on the bed, too, right next to me. She chatted with Pappy, who was lying in bed on the other side of the partition. She hummed drowsy hymns. She told us stories of when she was a little girl, and then stories of when Mammy Patsy and Uncle Jamesie and Uncle Leroy were little. And when she thought we were all asleep, she raised herself gently off the bed and left.

In the day she would come and sit on the chair by the bed, peeling vegetables, grating coconut, or picking rice, and talking, talking – about Ma Zelline and how she was still not too well, but how much she was looking forward to my visiting her when I got well; about how the mango-vert tree was bearing and Carlyle was eating all; about the big thanksgiving she was planning to keep because her granddaughter had been brought back to her...

Sometimes Pappy sat in the chair by the bed for hours, until he fell asleep on himself. Uncle Leroy would bring me a mango, or a ripe fig, and peel it for me. He would coax me to eat, telling me that he had just managed to save that one mango or that one ripe fig from Carlyle and the pigs. 'You better hurry up and come outside, you know, Lacey. They eating up everything!'

As the days passed, I began to realize that the house was overquiet. I could not hear Ruth and Kenwyn playing in the yard. Inside the house, the big-people talked in whispers. Sometimes Uncle Jamesie was there, and sometimes Tantie Monica; but I had not seen my cousins since the hospital.

Now I spent a lot of time straining my ears to pick up sounds from outside: the cocoyea broom scratching the ground; a hen singing loudly to let it be known that she had just laid her egg; Uncle Leroy calling Carlyle; a neighbour passing down the Trace and calling out greetings to Ma.

The quiet and the whispering began to annoy me. I was glad whenever the children came in to tell me their news: a big, bumpy *crapaud* had hopped into the kitchen and Ma chased it out with the cocoyea broom; Uncle Leroy was going to get watermelon for us; Carlyle had made mango chow for them, with hot, hot pepper; Ma couldn't find the frizzled fowl, so she must be setting in the bush. . .

By now I was able to run up and down the lines in the galvanize with no trouble at all. I took to sitting up on the bed to listen, instead of lying down with my eyes fixed on the roof.

Then one afternoon Ma and Pappy were talking in low voices in the gallery, and I heard Ma saying sadly that she couldn't bring Charlene for Easter with Lacey still so sick . . .

Slowly I climbed down from the bed. I stood for a few seconds to steady my legs – I had not walked for a long time.

When I appeared in the doorway, they were at first too shocked to move. Then Ma flew up and took hold of me. She led me to a chair, calling loudly all the while: 'Leroy! Leroy! Come quick, Leroy!'

Uncle Leroy came rushing around the side of the house with his cutlass in his hand. The dogs were right behind him, then Carlyle. Ruth and Kenwyn came up a few moments later. Kenwyn could not move very fast on his short bandy-legs, and Ruth had to wait for him.

I was glad to be in the world again. Every morning I got up early and went down to the kitchen with Ma and Pappy. They let me drink coffee with them – just a little drop, with plenty of milk – and we made chocolate tea for the little children. We kneaded the flour and fried little bakes, or we put one big bake to roast while we sipped our coffee.

At first they made me lie down and rest every afternoon, but after a few days I protested, because I was no longer sick or weak. I began to help Ma with the sugar-cake again.

Then when Charlene came I took over bathing the little children. At the end of each day they wore a coat of dust streaked with mango or some other juice, and their feet were often cased in mud. I would fetch some buckets of water and fill the bath pan in the back yard. When I had scrubbed, rinsed, and dried each one, I put them to sit on the back steps. They put their clothes on, and I sat on the steps and combed their hair while Ma or Uncle Leroy made tea down in the kitchen.

A few days before the end of the holidays, I put on Ma's boots and tied my head with a cloth to go down into the land with Uncle Leroy and Carlyle.

We walked past my garden, which was all in bush.

'Well, that is the end of the dolly-garden,' Uncle Leroy said. 'Now you going down and make *real* garden. You have to make garden to *eat* now, girl, because you not getting Mr Cephas grocery food again!'

Uncle Leroy had already explained to me that my father was still going to buy my books and uniform each year, but that was all. He refused to give money to help feed me, or to pay the taxi fare to Junction.

One day while I was still sick, Pappy, Uncle Jamesie and Uncle Leroy had gone to see my father in his office. They had told him that I could not live with him, but that he still had to help me, or I wouldn't be able to finish secondary school.

Uncle Leroy would not tell me what exactly had happened in the office, or how they had persuaded my father to help me.

'Oh, we just make him sweat a little bit' was all he would say, giving a wicked smile. 'Man, we coulda sweat out the taxi money out of he, you know – taxi money, lunch money, anything! But your dotish grandfather stop us, and make one big speech: "We have our pride and our dignity. You may keep your filthy lucre, man, and live with your conscience. We are thankful for small mercies. God will provide."'

Uncle Leroy's imitations of Pappy always made me laugh. We were sitting on the back steps, and I laughed so loudly that Ma poked her head through the kitchen window and peered up at us. A smile spread over her face: 'Well, hear you, eh girl? You *alive*!'

*

Early one morning the frizzled fowl came strutting into the yard with a noisy band of chickens behind her. Ma said that those chickens would be mine, and when the hens started to lay I could sell the eggs in the market so that I would have a little taxi fare.

She was not happy about my having to get up so early every morning to catch the bus. She called curses down on my father for his stinginess, and fretted to herself that she did not know how the child would make out – foreday morning the poor child would be on the road as though she was going to do estate work.

'Don't mind that, Ma,' I said. 'Anjanee used to have to wake up four o'clock in the morning to go to school.'

I thought about Anjanee a great deal. I wasn't afraid to think about her now. Sometimes I still dreamed that the two of us were on a bus together going somewhere, and talking, talking to each other.

As the reopening of school drew closer, I felt as though I was taking up her life. For just like her I would now have to set out early, early in the morning and travel miles to school. At home I would have plenty of work to do, and I would have to go and help with selling the things that Ma and Carlyle made during the week. We had to make ends meet, for we did not want to trouble Mammy Patsy for anything more than she was already sending us. She had to have her chance, too, and we would have to learn to cut and contrive, Ma said, so that Mammy Patsy would have money to go to school.

My thoughts went to La Puerta Government Secondary School, and to the Cephases. I felt very sorry for Michael. I decided that I would go and visit him one day, and Miss Velma, and even my father.

When I tried to think of Mrs. Lopez, all that came into my mind was Marlon Peters decked in all his sister's clothes, with his grandmother's stock-ings sliding down his legs. Then Mrs. Lopez became a Carnival character on Jouvert morning beating on an old rusty pitch-oil tin and making a long, incompre-hensible speech.

On the weekend before I went back to school, Uncle Leroy and his friends started to build the big bamboo tent in the yard for the thanksgiving. Ma was planning to feed everybody in Sooklal Trace as well as all her godchildren, *macommères*, relatives, friends, and enemies, it seemed. All the neighbours had already agreed to lend us chairs, and a whole gang of neighbours and *macommères* were going to come and help with the cooking.

The Saturday after the reopening of school was my birthday, and that was the day when Ma was going to keep the thanksgiving.